HOUDINI LIVES!

A NOVEL

BY

AL BLANCHARD
&
ADAM STEINFELD

ISBN: 978-0-6151-3583-0

Printed in the United States of America.

Book Cover Art design by MARK PARKER

THIS IS A NOVEL OF FICTION
With the exception of actual personages identified as such, the characters and incidents in the fictional novel are entirely the products of the authors imaginations and have no relation to any person or event in real life.

www.MagicLive.com
www.HoudiniLives.com

PREFACE

What if . . . Houdini didn't die back in 1926, and faked his own death? It's forty years later, the year 1966, and he's living in Miami Beach. What is he doing? Who are his friends? Will he ever return to magic?

I posed these questions to novelist Al Blanchard back in April 2002 in Aruba. Al was visiting the island with his lovely wife Enid. Back then, I presented my grand illusions magic show— Adam Steinfeld MagicLive!—nightly at the local beach casino, ending with the famous Houdini Water Torture tank (escaping from a tank filled with 200 lbs of freezing cold water while locked in chains).

Al handed me his business card. He said he liked the idea and told me to send him more on the story. So began my two-year odyssey. I was under contract to perform, and Al was in Boston, so much of the story drafts were e-mailed back and forth each day or week. My short story went from treatment to film script to the final novel before you.

Al always gave me great respect, even when I thought a few of the story concepts were too fantastic. It's fiction based on fact and ranges from comedy, to murder mystery, to political drama, to romance.

Al Blanchard, co-author, is the past president of the New England chapter of Mystery Writers of America, author of *Murder at Walden Pond*, the *Mad Season*, the *Iscariot Conspiracy*, the *Disappearance of Jenna Drago*, the *Stalker and Other Tales of Love and Murder*. *He is also author of Steve Asher and James Callahan* mystery series. He was in his prime as a writer, and then in an instant, he was taken away. Al was presiding over the third annual New

England Crimebake, doing what he most loved, when he died unexpectedly of an acute pulmonary embolism—only a few months after the novel and filmscript were completed—stunning the New England mystery writing community.

So, Ladies and Gentlemen, without further ado, I introduce Al Blanchard's lastest novel, and my second book. It's a tall tale of fun, murder, mystery, romance, and political drama with the world famous Houdini as the central character, joined by the upcoming young magician Stanford, who is determined to be rich and famous, and the lovely Solea, the magician's assistant. This story is mixed with a few historical characters of that time period, not to mention the political turmoil of a story set in 1966. Sit back, relax, and enjoy.

Adam Steinfeld, October 2006.

ACKNOWLEDGEMENTS

Many thanks to Al Blanchard, his wife Enid, and the wonderful island of Aruba, which allowed my imagination to run wild. And of course, the fantastic, all powerful Harry Houdini, who is discovered by every generation to be the greatest magician that ever lived—or as Sid Radner, the foremost authority on Houdini says, "another Houdini's excitement."

Adam Steinfeld

CONTENTS

PROLOGUE

Harry Houdini bounded onto the stage and bowed. He gazed out on the packed theater, his adrenaline at full throttle. A sense of pride enveloped him. It was a constant struggle to keep his name at the top of the playbill and sell out show after show, but he'd worked hard at it over the years and no one did it better. Tonight would be a more difficult performance than usual, but he was ready for it.

He slipped out of his blue velvet robe, letting it fall to the floor to reveal the one-piece bathing suit clinging to his muscular body. He'd always been annoyed by his height, but he made up for his five-four frame by constantly working out. He relished the oohs and aahs of the crowd when he posed and showcased his well-toned physique.

The pain in his abdomen still ached from where the college student had punched him. It was one of the few times in his career that a challenge had gone wrong. Before allowing anyone to hit his cast iron stomach, he'd always tensed his muscles, but the boy had caught him off guard and the pain still nagged.

The theater had been sold out for weeks, a far cry from his early days in Vaudeville when he played to half full houses if he was lucky. In Europe, he was loved and respected. It had only been recently that his United States audiences had grown. It took Americans longer to appreciate the rare talent he had.

He spread his hands and bowed again as the audience continued to applaud. There was nothing better than an appreciative crowd.

The house lights were dim, but he could still make out many of the spectators. They were mostly older and well dressed. An equal number of men and women, and even a few children, were in attendance. He wished his mother were still alive to see the adulation that was now heaped on him.

As the cheering subsided, his three male assistants walked onto the stage. Dressed in black striped pants and brocaded jackets, they were a sharp contrast to the magician, which was the effect he wanted. A hush fell over the crowd. Houdini knew that his final illusion would be spectacular, better than most could imagine.

"How have you enjoyed my performance so far?" He tried to keep his voice low, knowing it was higher pitched than most expected, but his grammar was flawless. During his early days in Vaudeville, hecklers had made fun of the way he spoke, and he'd worked hard to end that humiliation.

The spectators applauded louder than before.

"Ladies and gentlemen, let me introduce my original invention, The Water Torture Cell."

He pointed to a blue velvet curtain just as his assistants pulled it aside. The audience seemed to lean forward at once as they gazed at the five-foot high box, built of ornate mahogany wood, with a glass front and several slender steel bars on the inside. It was wide enough for a man of the magician's size to fit in. The top, with its sliding wooden panels, had been removed and rested on the floor several feet away. Extended from the ceiling was a hoist of chains and ropes used for lowering him into the cell.

He allowed the crowd a long look before continuing. He knew they'd heard many stories about this escape and wanted to increase the drama by remaining silent. He'd learned during his thirty plus years of performing that it was always better to let the audience's imagination run wild.

He studied the people in the front row for a moment before speaking. A few appeared startled, and others were wide-eyed with anxiety. "Although there is nothing supernatural about it, I am willing to forfeit the sum of one thousand dollars to anyone who can prove that it is possible to get air inside of the torture cell when I'm locked in it, in the regulation manner, after it has been filled with water."

A murmur passed through the spectators. He'd issued this

challenge many times and never had a taker, but his asking convinced the onlookers that the illusion was a fair one.

He waited for silence. "Should anything go wrong when I'm locked up, one of my assistants will be ready to demolish the glass, allowing the water to spill, in order to save my life." He turned to the men on stage with him. "You may now fasten my ankles to the top of the cell so that I may be lowered inside."

The audience appeared mesmerized, their eyes riveted on him. He bent low and stepped onto the lid of the cell. Months ago, he'd broken an ankle while performing this illusion. The pain had been excruciating, but he'd completed the show anyway. The mind had the ability to overcome many obstacles. He'd never let anything stop him from pleasing his fans.

He tensed his muscles as his ankles were locked into a device that looked much like the stocks of colonial times. Then buckets were used to fill the chamber with water until the level was within a few inches of the top of the glass front. He glanced into the wings and noted that everyone's attention was riveted on him. He studied them, realizing how much he'd miss show business when his career ended.

The assistants approached Houdini and surrounded him in a tight circle. He could sense their tension and almost smell their fear. He was the most relaxed man on stage because he knew what to expect. Even tonight.

The audience moved restlessly. "But there is no room in the chamber for you," someone yelled.

His eyes blazed and a slight smile crossed his face. He'd hoped someone from the audience would issue a challenge. It made the show more interesting.

A man dressed in a dark coat and top hat seated in the second row got up. "How do we know you're really securely fastened into the lid?" he yelled.

Houdini narrowed his eyes, trying to appear irritated, but he'd heard this question many times and welcomed it. "Come and check for yourself."

The man looked around, clearly delighted by the attention his remark had gotten. Dashing up the steps to the stage, he bent and tugged on the locks, and then he knocked on the wood of the lid. Lastly, he tried to move Houdini's feet.

Houdini fought hard to keep a look of amusement off his face. "Are you satisfied?"

The man pointed to the cell. "What if there's a trap door under it so you can escape?"

Houdini stood straighter, liking this man more with each question. "Select any part of the stage and my assistants will move the box."

The man walked slowly along the stage, tapping the floor with his shoe. Then he pointed to a spot a few feet away from where the chamber sat. "There."

The assistants slid the box across the floor.

"Is there anything else you'd like to check?" Houdini asked.

The man studied the chamber and knocked on the glass, the wood, and the steel. "You may proceed."

Houdini looked out toward the audience. "Would anyone else like to examine the locks or chamber?"

When no one responded, two assistants lifted Houdini and tilted him over the top of the cell, head down. He tightened his muscles and the familiar feeling of exertion and exhilaration passed through him. He wiggled as if fighting the chains and allowed a look of terror to cross his face. So much of magic was acting. He wanted the audience to believe he was in danger.

He studied the water below him and rattled the chains as the ropes tightened. He'd done this so many times it was almost relaxing. The third assistant put on a fireman's helmet, a rubber coat, and carried a red fire ax. He examined the glass closely, as if judging how much force to use in case something went wrong.

Then the curtain closed, blocking the audience's view of what was happening onstage.

Jimmy Wilson sat mesmerized as the water splashed onto the stage. In his fourteen years of life, he'd never spent a more thrilling afternoon. Houdini had been his idol for as long as he could remember, and when he heard the magician was coming to Detroit he'd begged his father to bring him.

And the show had been better than he could have imagined. How could a man do all those tricks? The most amazing thing had been when he swallowed dozens of needles and a bunch of thread and then pulled the needles from his mouth all threaded.

He'd been bored when Houdini talked about psychics, and he wished he'd walked through a wall or made an elephant disappear like he did in other shows, but Jimmy wasn't complaining. At least he was seeing the Water Torture Cell Escape.

The curtain opened and he got a brief view of the magician being lowered deeper as his assistants clamped the roof onto the cell with padlocks. Houdini wiggled and tugged as the water engulfed him, and Jimmy held his own breath. He wanted to match his ability with the great magician but didn't think he'd be able to hold it as long. Maybe when he got older he could. Then a curtain was drawn, shielding the box.

His dad leaned close to him. "Don't be scared, son. Houdini has done this many times."

Jimmy smiled at his father, feeling safe and knowing nothing could go wrong as long as they were together.

The orchestra played a song and his father said, "That song's called 'The Diver' and it was selected by Houdini to be played with this illusion."

Jimmy wished the music would stop. He'd like to hear the noises coming from behind the curtain. He tried to put himself in Houdini's mind and wondered what it would be like to be underwater.

Stars appeared on the edge of his vision, and he let out his breath. He'd have to practice at home to get better. The people around him stared at the stage. No one seemed worried, and his dad was actually smiling.

Jimmy fidgeted in his seat. *Wow,* he thought. Houdini could really hold his breath for a long time.

Suddenly a scream came from behind the curtain. "Get him out," someone yelled. The music stopped. Glass shattered and water flooded the stage, gushing under the curtain and into the orchestra pit, scattering the musicians. The audience gasped and Jimmy jumped up. He couldn't see over the man in front of him. He darted down his row, tripping over legs and feet, and out into the aisle. Was this part of the act? A velour curtain dropped down, blocking the entire stage from view. The silence around him frightened him and as the seconds passed, Jimmy knew that something had gone terribly wrong.

THE NEXT MORNING

A young boy held a stack of newspapers as he walked down a busy roadway. He thrust one into the air. "Extra. Extra. Houdini Dead. Read all about it. A horrible tragedy at the Garrick. Houdini dies performing trick. Read all about it."

MACHPEHLA CEMETARY – CYPRESS HILLS, L.I., NEW YORK
TWO DAYS LATER

It was a dark, overcast day. The air smelled of rain, but none had fallen yet. Mourners, wearing heavy coats to shield them from the cold, trudged by a solid bronze coffin shrouded by a white lambskin, purple violets, and garlands of southern smilax. Thousands had packed the sidewalks of New York City to watch the procession of twenty-five automobiles and the casket pass by on its way to the cemetery.

The line at the gravesite snaked out onto the street and down the road, a fitting tribute to the great entertainer. Most people were quiet and solemn; some were crying and others clutched a picture of Houdini. The burial plot was between his parents and inside the casket was a parcel of his mother's letters, which Houdini had requested be buried with him.

Rabbi Tinter of Mount Zion Temple completed the eulogy and explained Jewish burial customs for those unaware. A few people took a shovelful of dirt and threw it on the casket as they left the graveside. Then the crowd broke into two lines and Bess, Houdini's wife, made her way through it, accepting condolences. She looked frail and her eyes were tear-rimmed. The couple had been inseparable for so many years and the strain of the past few days was showing on her face.

As the crowd dispersed, a woman looked at the male mourner next to her. "There will never be another Houdini. I can't believe he's dead."

The man nodded. "Neither can I. At least he died the way he wanted, performing in front of an audience. I keep expecting to turn around and see him standing there telling us this was another of his publicity stunts. You do know that he built the casket he's in?"

"What are you saying?"

"The coffin was constructed for a trick and would be a simple box for Houdini to escape from. He was buried alive many times in it and got out unscathed."

The woman shook her head and gazed back at the casket. "Hundreds witnessed his death. Face it. The great magician is dead."

The man lowered his voice. "But why wasn't an autopsy performed? Don't you find that strange?"

The woman was about to respond when a gust of wind picked up and rain cascaded down on the mourners. Black umbrellas fluttered open and people quick-stepped toward their cars, a mixture of Bentleys, Model-T's, and Chevrolets.

On a hill overlooking the cemetery, standing in the shadows of a giant oak tree, a man stared down at the crowd. He was dressed in a heavy black topcoat with a fedora pulled close to his eyes. His coat billowed in the wind.

The male mourner spotted him and pointed to the figure. "Look. Do you see that man? He seems so familiar. It almost looks like . . ."

The woman followed his gaze.

The figure skittered behind the tree.

The woman scrunched her eyes, staring. The tree branches swayed. No one was visible to her—then a flash of movement at the periphery of her vision, moving quickly away. All around her, everything grew still, and even the birds were quiet.

"Oh my God," she said. "You're right. He did look like Houdini. You don't think . . . No, impossible. Maybe it's his spirit. He always said he'd come back from the dead." The woman turned back and tilted her chin toward the freshly dug grave. "Houdini is in that casket. That's one thing I'm certain of."

The man stared into the woman's eyes. "Are you? Nothing with Houdini is as it seems. What if Houdini does live?"

"But why would he pretend to die?" the woman asked. "It doesn't make sense. And if he did fake his death, what in the world does he plan to do next?"

1

THE GREAT STANFORD MEETS SOLEA

Stanford took a sip of his Coke and then wedged the bottle into the white sand so it wouldn't topple. His white shorts and tie-dye San Francisco tee shirt stuck to his body from the heat, and sweat dripped down his face. A dozen beautiful women in skimpy, colorful bathing suits played volleyball on the beach. He watched a tall blonde spike the ball to end the game. Life didn't get much better, but he couldn't just stand around gawking. It was time to go after what he'd really come for.

He glanced at the blue Atlantic and watched the waves in the distance glisten, peak, and then break apart into white swirls as they meandered toward the sandy shore. The scene reminded him of his home in California. Florida was nice, but he wasn't sure he'd ever get used to the humidity.

During his two weeks in Miami, he'd performed his magic act in several local clubs on Collins Ave, and his hard work and willingness to do anything for publicity was beginning to pay off. At twenty-five, he was younger than most magicians performing in the area, and his energy level had no limit.

Not only was he a great illusionist but he'd recently added music to his act. And not that ancient stuff that the old timers played, but new songs by the Beatles, The Byrds, The Rolling Stones, and Bob Dylan. He did his tricks with a flourish to the loud Rock 'n Roll music he loved. This got him attention, particularly from younger club goers, and if there was one thing he'd learned over the years, it was that an entertainer had to set himself apart from all others.

When he was thirteen, he'd decided to become a magician after watching a movie about Houdini starring Tony Curtis and Janet Leigh. The old magician was cool and seemed able to do anything. Stanford's curiosity about how his illusions were done led him to magic. As an adult, he included some of them in his act as a tribute to the man who'd hooked him on magic.

As an only child growing up outside of L.A., he'd had plenty of time to practice. While a teenager, he put on shows for neighborhood kids and charged them money to attend. Then he'd invest every cent in newer and flashier tricks. In high school, he'd performed in talent shows. He found his magic attracted girls, and the loneliness he'd felt growing up quickly evaporated as more people paid attention to him. When he turned eighteen and most of his friends went off to college, he'd gone to San Francisco to perform magic on the streets and then passed a hat to eat and pay the rent. He'd always had an independent streak, so going off alone to a strange city was exciting to him. It was a tough time, but he never thought of giving up.

San Francisco is where he got his first break. The producer of a local television program spotted him and booked him on his show. That one appearance turned to several, but after a few months, San Francisco became too confining for him. His restless streak made him move on. He wanted to see the country.

He'd gone to Seattle, Portland, Santa Fe, and across a lot of the western states playing local clubs. Those open mikes where he'd been on the bill with off key singers, humorless comedians, jittery jugglers, and anyone else with guts enough to take the stage, whether they had talent or not, toughened him and made him realize how hard it would be to reach his goal. It made him stronger and more determined.

During those years on the road, he'd learned to handle hecklers, drunks who threw things, and crowds who didn't pay attention. He realized he could win over any audience with charm, talent, and cockiness.

Next to New York City, Miami was a Mecca for a performer, which is why he'd stopped here, doing shows in many local clubs. It was at one of those gigs that he'd met Rabbi Weiss, an older and well-known Rabbi in the area. Weiss had come to watch him perform and was so impressed he'd offered him a job as a headliner for a gala fundraiser he was putting on in a week. This was Stanford's chance to make a name for himself with the rich and elite of Miami. It would be his biggest gig, and he vowed to make it his best. Who knew where it could lead?

But all professional magicians had a beautiful assistant, which was why he was on the beach checking out the women in the skimpy bathing suits. Well, it wasn't the only reason.

He approached the blonde woman who had ended the volleyball game with a spike. He smiled, reached behind her ear, and pulled out a quarter. "Did you lose this?"

The woman's eyes widened. "Hey, how'd you do that?"

He turned to another woman and performed the same stunt. Then he handed a bracelet back to a woman who'd been wearing it around her wrist. All of these were routine sleight of hand tricks guaranteed to attract a crowd.

Within minutes, a dozen women and a few men surrounded him. Although they wanted to see more, he hadn't come here to do magic.

He surveyed the crowd and gave them a toothy grin before speaking. He knew that with his blonde beach boy looks and dimpled chin, some claimed he looked like a young Kirk Douglas. "I'm The Great Stanford. Most of you have never heard of me, but you may look back on this day as one that changed your life, for I can guarantee you that shortly I'll be known as the world's greatest magician."

The crowd stared, more interested now. A few snickered at his self-confidence, but no one left. He had their attention, and he worked them just as he would any audience at one of his shows.

"I've performed magic for a number of years alone, and it's time for me to take an assistant. This could be your lucky day." He smiled again. "I need a beautiful young woman who's interested in magic to work with me. This is an unbelievable opportunity for the right person. Any one of you is gorgeous enough to fill the role. I'll train you in all aspects of magic so all you need is a minimum of dexterity. The pay isn't much, but you'll get to travel across this great country and perform in some of the best theaters. Many important people attend my shows, so who knows what might happen. Come on, ladies. Show me what you can do."

Stanford made eye contact with each woman. He knew what

he'd told them wasn't true, but he felt strongly that once people saw him perform at the fundraiser, it would be.

A brunette raised her hand. Stanford handed her a deck of cards. "Shuffle those for me, please?"

She crouched on the sand and fumbled with the cards. A few flipped wildly onto the ground.

Stanford smiled. "You've just flunked the audition. Would anyone else like to try?"

One by one, women came forward and tried to perform tricks. They mishandled cards, dropped coins, and flirted with Stanford. He shook his head after each performance. *Sure, they're beautiful,* he thought, *but I need someone who is trainable.* Finding the right person wasn't going to be easy.

He noticed a big black man jogging along the beach followed by four other men and immediately recognized him.

"Hey," he called out. "I know you. You're the greatest heavyweight champion of all time."

Cassius Clay stopped jogging, ran in place for a few seconds, and then shadow boxed toward Stanford. "I float like a butterfly and sting like a bee." He eyed the women. "Why are all these beautiful women around you? You're scrawny and ugly. Everyone knows I am the prettiest." He jabbed his thumb toward his chest. "You ladies should be with me."

Stanford got irritated, not from the insult but because the women now seemed more interested in the boxer than him.

"I'm The Great Stanford, a magician. I bet the ladies would be impressed if you helped me perform one of my tricks."

Clay grinned. "I'm the greatest, not you." He clenched his fist, pulled his arm back, then moved it forward quickly to within a few inches of Stanford's face. Stanford didn't flinch.

"My biggest trick is making the best heavyweights disappear."

"And predicting the round," Stanford said. "Magic requires dexterity, athleticism, and courage. It's just like boxing."

The magician balled his hand, then stuffed a red silk handkerchief into the fist. After a moment, he opened his hand and waved his fingers. The handkerchief disappeared.

Clay scrunched his eyes, feigned a look of shock, and jogged in place. "You're not bad. Can you fight?"

Stanford smiled. "I leave boxing to the professionals. I bet you'd be good performing magic. Why don't you show me your stuff?"

"I can do anything. Give me those cards. I'll show you a trick."

Stanford handed him the deck. "You realize that I am to magic what you are to boxing."

"Kid, I like your attitude. Thing is, five years from now no one will know who you are. I'll still be heavyweight champ, and you'll be waiting tables down at the Fontainebleau."

Clay took the cards, shuffled them, and then held out the deck. "Pick a card, close your eyes, and concentrate on your card."

Stanford selected one, studied it, put it back in the deck, and closed his eyes. He knew there was no way the champ could figure out what card he'd selected and looked forward to the expression on the man's face when he guessed wrong.

Clay walked to the water and scattered the deck into the pounding surf. "Okay, kid. You can look now."

Stanford opened his eyes, clearly confused.

Clay pointed toward the ocean and the cards floating on top of the water. "Here's a life lesson for you. Don't ever close your eyes to a champion."

Clay jogged away, followed by his entourage. Three young boys scampered into the water, squealing and picking up the cards.

Stanford watched Clay disappear up the beach. Although the champ had made him look foolish, he knew that people would be talking about what happened. Any publicity was good.

He noted a beautiful woman, probably in her early twenties, on the edge of the crowd. She wore a skimpy bikini, which showed off her voluptuous body. Her hair was dark, curly, and very long. It broke on thin shoulders at the curve of her breasts. Her eyes were near black and her lips were full and painted in deep red. She smiled at him and walked slowly along the beach. Then she glanced back. Was it his imagination or did she want him to notice her?

Stanford jogged to catch up. "Hey, where are you going so fast? Don't you want to see some magic?"

She continued along the beach, quickening her pace. "Magic? Since when is it considered magic to have your cards thrown into the water?"

"Oh, he was just playing with me. A joke among fellow

professionals. Let me teach you some sleight of hand. It's simple. You'll be able to amaze your friends."

She glanced at him, and then looked away. "That was Cassius Clay, wasn't it?"

"It was. Are you a boxing fan?"

"No, I abhor it, but he is a beautiful man. And so strong."

"Ah. But is he clever like me? I'm looking for an assistant in my act. Why didn't you audition like the others?"

The woman studied him for a moment, not breaking stride. "You were surrounded by those beautiful women. I didn't want to disturb you."

"None were as beautiful as you."

The woman shook her head, a look of amusement on her face. "Are you this forward with everyone?"

Out of the corner of his eye, Stanford noticed a man in a white knit shirt and black trunks who seemed to be following and listening. When he looked over, the man turned away. The guy looked vaguely familiar. Maybe it was someone Stanford had seen at one of his shows.

He refocused on the woman. "I'm from California. We're all forward there. My name is Stanford. My stage name is The Great Stanford."

"I am Solea." Her eyes twinkled. "I have no stage name."

"Solea is beautiful enough. Do you live in Miami?"

"Yes. I've only been in America a few months. I came from Barcelona."

"Barcelona? Really? I've always dreamed of visiting Spain."

"The country is beyond description. I have relatives all over Spain. My father died years ago, but my mother saved her money to send me to America. This is the land of opportunity, she told me, where everyone's dream comes true. She loved your President Kennedy."

"He was a great man. His death tore this country apart. I don't know if we'll ever be the same. Are you living here by yourself?"

"My uncle took me in, but it's time for me to be on my own. I've been thinking of traveling. Maybe I'll visit your California."

"It's a gorgeous state." He hesitated. "You know, this could be the day that changes your life. You saw me auditioning those women for my assistant's job. Would you like to be in show business? You'd be able to travel all across America with me."

"You're offering me a job? Don't you want me to perform a trick like the others? What do you Americans call it? An audition?"

"It's not necessary. I know you'll be perfect. Come away with me."

Solea scrunched her eyes. "You're crazy. My mother warned me to watch out for American men who would promise to take me places. She said they might try to take advantage of me."

Stanford glanced behind her. The man in the white knit shirt was several feet away gazing out onto the ocean. Something about the expression on his face made Stanford uneasy.

Stanford put his hand on Solea's shoulder and she stopped walking. The wind swept her hair back. "Of course I'm crazy. If I wasn't I wouldn't be a magician, but do I look like the type of man who'd take advantage of a beautiful woman?"

Solea tilted her head and smiled. "The real question is would I take advantage of you?"

Stanford smiled. "I like you. You're a wild one. You and I would be great on stage together. Someday I'm going to be the most famous magician of all time."

"Greater than Houdini?"

"People will speak of The Great Stanford and Houdini in the same breath."

Solea glanced at two men passing a football. She seemed deep in thought. "You are very ambitious."

"One thing I learned long ago is you never get what you want unless you go after it. It's all timing, patience, and luck. Talent doesn't hurt in the show business game either, but that's something you can develop through hard work."

"You seem very impressed with yourself."

"I know what I'm capable of doing. I'm young and have my whole life ahead of me."

They started walking again and stepped around an elderly couple sitting in the sand. Solea's expression turned serious. "And what is it you want out of life, Great Stanford?"

"Fame, fortune, and for you to be my assistant."

She giggled and for an instant looked much younger than her years. "I know nothing about magic. I am a singer. My uncle said I am very good."

"Well, maybe we can add one of your songs to the act. As my assistant, all you'd have to do is look beautiful and distract the crowd. That's something you accomplish without even trying. And, of course, you'd have to spend a lot of time with me."

"I don't know if it would be possible to spend time with someone as egotistical as you."

"There's a difference between being egotistical and working hard to be the best."

"I like men who are laid back. Being with you might be difficult."

"I think you could get used to it. I know I could certainly get used to being with you. Have dinner with me tonight and we can discuss it."

Solea waved her hand toward the ocean. It might have been Stanford's imagination, but he thought she locked eyes with the man in the white knit shirt for an instant and gave him a brief smile.

"Anyone on the beach would want to be with you. Why choose me?"

"No one is as beautiful as you."

Solea jabbed a finger at him. "You are exactly the type of American my mother warned me about. I must admit, however, you are very handsome. I will have dinner with you, but I make no promise about the future."

Stanford took Solea's hand. When he looked for the man he'd felt was following him, the guy had disappeared.

OCTOBER 1966, WOLFIE'S DELI, MIAMI BEACH – LARRY KING SHOW

Larry King leaned forward and tapped the microphone. He glanced out toward the main room of the restaurant, taking in the mauve leather booths surrounded by pictures of Hollywood stars. Photos of Frank Sinatra, Judy Garland, Van Johnson, and the rotund man seated next to him, Jackie Gleason, adorned the walls. The Deli was a good example of Miami kitsch. Wolfie Cohen, the owner, had opened the place in the 1940s, coming from New York as part of that state's immigration to the Miami area. People flocked here for bagels and corned beef. Cohen was proud of the pink and blue décor and of the big names who made stopping at his establishment a ritual when they played the glamorous hotels on Miami Beach.

Smiling at Gleason, King said, "You gonna give me something good tonight, Jackie?"

Gleason was a large man, dressed in a navy suit, baby blue shirt, and a teal tie. He puffed on his cigarette, then took it out of his mouth and jabbed it toward King. "When have I ever let you down, buddy? Tonight I'm going to let your listeners in on a special secret. It's an exclusive just for you."

"Ten seconds, Mr. King," said a technician standing a few feet away.

The table was cluttered with coffee cups, water glasses, and an overstuffed ashtray. A few patrons of the Deli glanced over, knowing better than to interrupt. Larry King had broadcast his radio show from the same back booth for years. Many patrons came to see the celebrities being interviewed.

The technician pointed and King leaned even closer to the microphone. His suspenders wrinkled his white shirt. He slicked back his hair and adjusted his horn-rimmed glasses as if his listeners could see him. "Welcome to the Larry King Show. My guest tonight is the world's greatest comedian, Jackie Gleason. Thanks for stopping by, Jackie."

Gleason took a final drag on his cigarette, waved the smoke away with his hand, and stubbed the butt out in the ashtray. "Always a pleasure doing your show. How 'bout picking up the tab for my food tonight?"

King laughed. "I'd consider it as long as you don't eat until you're full."

"Wolfie doesn't have that much food." Gleason glanced at the man leaning against a wall and smiling. "Do ya, Wolfie?"

"Now, Jackie," King said. "I need you on your best behavior tonight."

"Life is too short for good behavior."

"You've been on my show many times, but there's one thing I've always wanted to ask you. You've done it all: movies, television, records, and now you've got the number one rated TV program. How do you do it?"

Gleason smiled. "Just a tribute to the public's good taste and my good looks. Actually I'll let you in on a secret. The key is always give the audience something they don't expect."

"You're right there. Okay, let's get to why you're really here tonight. You've got a special event planned for Halloween you want to tell us about."

Gleason adjusted his sport jacket, which looked like it might have fit twenty pounds ago. "I'm doing a TV special on magic. Many of the greatest magicians of all time will perform their amazing tricks and illusions. We're still finalizing the guest list, but some of these people haven't appeared in public for years. It'll be the greatest tribute to magic ever. That night marks the fortieth anniversary of the death of Harry Houdini, who was absolutely the best of them all. I'm hoping to have a big surprise for the viewing audience. It'll be more entertaining than watching *Lost in Space*."

King pushed back his glasses. "Your show is always a great take, but this sounds like a night not to be missed. Houdini has always fascinated me, and you have a great interest in him as well. We all know he claimed he'd make contact with us from the grave after his death. Many psychics tried to reach him and failed. Didn't he leave a special code with his wife so she'd know any message was really from him?"

"He did. 'Roseabelle believe' were the words, and some psychics claimed to have received this message from Houdini, but all of them proved to be hoaxes."

"Are you planning on contacting Houdini on your show?"

Gleason forced a smile, but didn't answer. There was something in his expression King couldn't read. He'd interviewed the comedian many times and it wasn't like him not to respond to a question. He wondered what was bothering his friend.

King quickly spoke, trying to fill in the silence. "Maybe Houdini was waiting for the right spot to make his appearance, like a top rated television show. Knowing how the man always liked to pull publicity stunts, I wouldn't put it past him. Or you."

Gleason turned serious. "If anyone can give us a message from the grave, it would be Houdini. He said many times if there was any way to do it, he would. My show will be televised live, and all I can say right now is people should tune in. If things work out the way I hope, they're in for a big surprise. Bigger than anything they could ever imagine. Everyone will be talking about this show for years. You certainly don't want to miss it."

King pointed a finger at Gleason. "It's unlike you to be so mysterious."

"The whole show will be mysterious. The last few years have been marked by unbelievable tragedies. My show will be the event that will cheer everyone up. I'm sworn to secrecy about what's going to take place. I wish I could be more open. You know what a big mouth I have."

King studied the big man. What in the world did he have planned and why wouldn't he talk about it? All he knew was that he'd never seen Gleason so serious.

2

I AM RABBI WEISS

The ornate theater was packed. A chandelier hung over the well-dressed audience and the carved mahogany wood on the walls gave the room an elegant feel. Some of the biggest stars in the world had appeared here. On stage, a podium sat off to the right. A man dressed in a dark blue suit, with a white shirt and dark tie, stood over it. He was a short man with a long beard and thinning gray hair. He appeared to be in his late seventies, but with his trim, athletic body and alert eyes, he could have been younger. A Yarmulke was on his head.

The man smiled gave a penetrating gaze toward the crowd. "For those of you who don't know me, I am Rabbi Weiss. Thank you for coming to my twelfth annual fund-raiser. This year we are raising money for the new Variety Children's Hospital and by coming you are helping and I couldn't continue my work without you. It's always a wonderful thing to aid those less fortunate, and as a Rabbi here in Miami for almost forty years, I have tried to show leadership by example. Tonight you'll be happy to know I have no sermon to give." He smiled as the crowd laughed. "I've always felt that magic is the greatest form of entertainment. Not as difficult to perform as getting you to donate money to one of my causes, but a close second. It's my pleasure tonight to introduce a magician who truly amazed me. I recently saw him perform and was very, very impressed. He's young and although I may have trouble with his clothes, the slang he uses when he talks, and that noise he calls music, I respect him for his ability to

13

perform magical feats of illusion. I feel he has a great future. I would give him one piece of advice, however. I think he should get a haircut." He paused. "Please welcome The Great Stanford."

The magician jogged onto the stage dressed in black pants and a tight red silk shirt with puffy sleeves. He was tall, slender, and in his mid-twenties with a Beatle-style haircut. His blue eyes, angular features, and the pronounced dimple in his chin gave him the appearance of a young kid in a rock band. As he gazed out onto the audience, he appeared self-assured, almost cocky.

He waved his hand toward the wing. "Please welcome my beautiful assistant, Solea."

A woman, who looked all of nineteen, with long flowing brown hair, elegant high cheekbones, and dark skin emphasizing her Spanish descent, walked out. Her short skirt revealed long, muscular, and shapely legs.

Stanford smiled. "I want to thank Rabbi Weiss for allowing me to perform for you tonight. What I'm going to do will amaze and challenge you. Prepare to be entertained."

Rabbi Weiss watched from offstage, a trace of jealousy passing through him. He picked two books up from the table next to him and cradled them in his arms. His eyes narrowed as Stanford began his act. "The boy has potential," he whispered to a stagehand standing next to him.

"I don't know about that," the stagehand said, "but his assistant sure is a looker."

Weiss looked at the woman. "She should be more modest, but her movements are quick and agile. She pulls attention from Stanford, which as any good magician knows is beneficial."

"You seem to know a lot about magic, Rabbi," the stagehand said.

Weiss nodded and as the stagehand walked away muttered to himself, "Maybe it's time."

THE SAND BEACH MOTEL – THREE BLOCKS FROM THE THEATER

The Sand Beach Motel was not one of Miami's premiere beach accommodations. It was a place for drifters or people who only wanted to spend an hour or two. Built in the early thirties, its run down appearance indicated it had never been remodeled. But the two men inside room nine didn't intend to sleep there. By morning, they hoped to be far away and very rich.

The room was small, with peeling paint and a mattress that sagged. A small black and white television set was chained to the chipped bureau, as if anyone would attempt to steal the outdated machine. A clock on the wall read 8:30. The large brown radio on the night table blared an Elvis song.

Renaldo Gomez took his .45 out of his shoulder holster, examined it closely, and then put it back. *One must check and recheck everything before doing a job,* he thought. He tugged on his dark sport jacket to make sure there were no wrinkles to reveal his weapon.

He glanced at the other man in the room. "It's going to be a marvelous night for us, Jared. One we will always remember. How often is a man able to say that?"

Renaldo was a heavyset Cuban American approaching forty. He had long sideburns and a pompadour haircut similar to Elvis Presley, his idol, to whom he bore a slight resemblance. He licked his full lips and pushed a wisp of his brown hair behind his ear.

He'd come to America ten years ago from Cuba searching for the American dream. After two years of unemployment, he'd hooked on with a gang of refugees that ran numbers and sold drugs. He made sure anyone who owed them money paid. He was good at it because he enjoyed inflicting pain on others. Occasionally he did an odd job on his own. The word was out that he'd do anything for a fast buck. It was his recklessness, marked with cruelty, that got him noticed. His reputation had grown in recent years.

He jabbed a finger at Jared. "Everything must happen quickly and precisely, as we planned. The element of surprise will make this an easy job. We can't afford to be even a few minutes off. If you follow my instructions implicitly, we'll be at some bar drinking beer just in time to see the results of our work on the news tonight."

Jared paced nervously. He was thirty with longish brown hair. His medium build and soft-spoken manner didn't give him a threatening appearance, which was an asset. He'd blend right into the crowd. Dressed in an identical sport jacket as his cousin Renaldo, he appeared less sure of what they were about to do. But he'd always been the more cautious of the two.

The song switched to Percy Sledge, and Renaldo sang the

15

opening words. "When a man loves a woman," he crooned, scrunching his eyes closed. He pointed to the radio. "Percy's good, but he's no Elvis."

Jared stopped pacing. "What's with this singing? We've got a serious situation ahead of us. Maybe we should run through it one more time just to make sure we have it right."

A look of annoyance crossed Renaldo's face. "We've done it a hundred times. The important thing is for me to get a clear shot at the magician, and the way I've mapped things out, that'll be easy. All you have to do is follow my lead and make sure no one attempts to stop me."

"You make it sound simple."

Renaldo put his hand on Jared's shoulder, the fondness he felt for the man evident from his expression. "You worry too much. Besides, we're being paid well for this job, and I'd like to be around to spend the money. And we will be. What will you do with your share?"

Jared took a long breath and his shoulders relaxed. "I'd like to open a restaurant. Not one of those cheap Cuban places that are found all over Miami, but a good one where a man will be proud to take his woman."

Renaldo touched one of his sideburns. "And you'll do that. Maybe with my share I'll buy one of those pink Cadillacs like Elvis owns. What's that song he sings? 'All Shook Up?' We'll be shaking up Miami tonight. Someday I hope to be as rich as Elvis. Ahh . . . the American dream where everybody owns a big car and a house. It's not like Cuba, my friend." Renaldo belched loudly. "I shouldn't have had that second hot dog. Now I have indigestion. But hot dogs are part of the American dream, too."

"Do you know what Americans put in hot dogs?"

"Don't tell me. I don't want to know."

Jared started to pace again. "How can you be so calm? I keep thinking something will go wrong."

"That won't happen. Everything has been planned to the final detail because if we fail it would mean our lives. You've met the man who hired us. Something in his eyes tells me we'd better succeed. That's certainly motivation to do the job. Besides, it's an honor that he selected us for this important job. When we show him how capable we are, he'll throw more work our way. He is a great man. He will, as Americans like to say, become our meal ticket." Renaldo smiled. "Maybe I'll buy two Cadillacs. Maybe someday our meal ticket will introduce me to Elvis. That would be a dream come true for me."

Jared walked to the mirror and adjusted his dark tie. "Why would Elvis want to meet you?"

"Because, my friend, we are both successful at what we do. He as an entertainer, and I at following orders from very wealthy men. Whatever those orders are. And I succeed each time, so don't worry. You stick with me, and we'll be living the dream our parents in Cuba told us about."

"It's just that there will be so many people. You say we will escape in the confusion, but I'm not so sure. Suppose the crowd attacks us. There are only two of us against so many."

"Trust me, Jared."

"Oh, sure. You're the one who said the Bay of Pigs invasion would be successful."

Renaldo heaved a long sigh. "Why must you be so negative? Was Elvis negative when he walked into that recording studio in Memphis to make a record for his mother? Of course not. He knew he was destined for greatness. The Americans bungled the Bay of Pigs. If they'd left us alone, we would have overthrown Castro. Successful people always think positively."

"Successful people don't attempt things that have so little margin for error."

Renaldo narrowed his eyes. "Don't make me have second thoughts about you. I included you on this because you are my cousin and in need of money. You were a tough kid growing up in Havana. You had to be strong because after the death of your father you were the man of the family. I was happy when I heard you were in Miami, but the curse of America is that a man can grow soft and lose his edge because of the money and women within his grasp. That would never happen to my Elvis. He will always maintain his edge, as I will. You haven't grown soft in the two years you've been here have you?"

Jared stood straighter. "You don't have to worry about me. It's my nature to want all angles covered. I just wonder if there's any other way to take the magician out."

"None. Don't you think I've considered other options? He's always on guard when by himself. The past attempts on his life have made him careful."

Jared looked away, the uncertainty still on his face.

Simon and Garfunkel's "Sounds of Silence" came through the radio speakers. "Wimp song," Renaldo said. "Those boys have no soul." He touched Jared's shoulder. "I have soul, cousin. That's what sets me apart from losers. The magician will never suspect anyone would go after him this way. He feels safe. That's the beauty of my plan and in the confusion, after the gunshots, we will get away."

"I hope you're right, Renaldo."

"Have you ever known me to be wrong? In the words of one of my hero's songs, we're going to have some Good Rockin' Tonight." He checked his watch. "The show will be ending shortly. It's time to Rock 'n Roll."

3
WE'RE BOUND TO FAIL

Weiss studied Stanford. The young magician started with simple sleight of hand tricks. Then he'd asked if anyone in the audience had a pair of handcuffs. Weiss smiled. That type of bluff had been a staple of Houdini's act. Who took a pair of handcuffs to the theater? The man who produced them was a plant. Stanford had his wrists cuffed behind his back. He could have been out of them in seconds, but prolonged his escape for the benefit of the audience. The pained expression and tugging of arms was all meant to make the spectators feel the magician was defeated. Weiss shook his head as fragmented memories flooded back to him.

Stanford moved professionally through the rest of his act, drawing each illusion out until the precise moment when the audience felt things had gone wrong. The levitation and sawing of his lovely assistant in half were all basic to magic. Weiss knew how each trick was performed, but still enjoyed watching.

The audience erupted in wild applause as Stanford completed his final illusion. The young magician bowed, smiled, and waved a hand toward Solea. Then he exited the stage, waited a beat, and walked back out holding his arms in the air like a victorious boxer.

Rabbi Weiss watched in amusement. When the magician came off the stage, he shook his hand and patted him on the shoulder.

"What a buzz," Stanford said. "There's nothing like having total command of an audience like that. My adrenaline is still pumping. I won't be able to sleep for hours."

"You were wonderful," Weiss said. "Even better than the last time I saw you perform. I must say I'm very impressed that someone so young has such a command of the stage."

"Thanks, man. I'm glad you enjoyed the show. It's hard work, but I love it. I couldn't imagine doing anything else. Usually I use a little music to fire up the audience. You know, some Beatles, Byrds, or maybe 'Wild Thing' by the Troggs. But, this being a religious fundraiser, I understand why you didn't want me to use any."

"A true magician's job is to mystify as cleverly and dramatically as possible. The great ones don't need music. Your show is spectacular without it." Weiss looked out at the emptying theater feeling exhilarated, as if he'd been on stage performing. "Your agility is top rate. You must have started doing magic as a young child."

Stanford wiped a bead of perspiration from his forehead. "I was thirteen when I saw a film about Houdini. It was the most wonderful thing I'd ever seen in my short lifetime. I knew right then I wanted to be a magician. I couldn't learn magic fast enough. Other kids my age were surfing and learning to play the guitar so they could pick up chicks, but not me."

Weiss remembered the film starring Tony Curtis as the great magician. The film was mostly fiction and certainly didn't do justice to the greatness that was Houdini.

"You grew up in California, right? It must have been hard to get the proper training there."

"Nah. Not when you want something as badly as I wanted this. I'd stay in my room and practice four or five hours a day. I'd read every book on magic I could get my hands on. Those tricks are second nature to me, but they do amaze the crowd." He glanced out at the people slowly walking up the aisle and toward the lobby. "This is quite a gig you have here. If you want me back next year, all you have to do is ask."

Weiss noticed Solea standing close by. He wondered why she didn't go to her dressing room. Was it his imagination or was she intent on overhearing them? Were they a couple? The Spanish beauty and the young, good-looking magician seemed an unlikely pair, but who could understand this new generation.

Weiss cradled the two books in his arms. "I admired your ability to deceive the crowd but even more impressive was your showmanship. With a stage act like that, you'll go far in the world of magic. Of course, it will take many years of study. It's not something that comes easily. You must constantly find new and better tricks so you don't become stale. You must publicize yourself and create an aura of mystery."

Stanford looked at Weiss in surprise. "Sounds to me like you know a little about magic."

"I did study the craft a little. A magician creates a world of wonder and asks people to enter and believe in that world. It's the highest form of entertainment. As a token of my admiration for you, I would like to loan you two books about the greatest magician of all time." He handed the books to Stanford. "Harry Houdini. You did say he is your inspiration."

Stanford took the books and studied the covers. His face broke into a wide grin. "Thanks, man. Houdini was hip."

"Hip?"

"Yeah, he marched to his own drumbeat. No one was going to tell him what to do. I admired that."

"Houdini would admire you as well. I noticed that you incorporated a few of his illusions into your act."

"I only steal from the best, Rabbi."

"You do have Houdini's desire to succeed."

"You've got that right. I won't let anything get in the way of what I want. Hey, you criticized my use of music. Houdini always had an orchestra playing when he performed, didn't he?"

Weiss pointed to the books. "Houdini did many things. As you'll read, he was more than an ordinary man. He was a wonderful showman and a scholar on many subjects. I could tell by your act that you were a great admirer of him."

"Absolutely. He was a personal hero of mine. You wanna hear something funny? I always figured Houdini would come back from the dead. That he'd figure out a way to communicate with us and let us know what the afterlife was all about."

An amused expression crossed Weiss's face. "It's been forty years. Surely if Houdini was going to do something, he'd have done it by now. From my knowledge of the magician, he wasn't a very patient man."

"Forty years is an eyelash flicker in dead years. I still have hopes Houdini will put in an appearance from the grave. That would be his greatest trick and insure that his legend will live forever."

21

Weiss stood straighter. "Oh, I think his legend will live forever anyway. I'd like to talk to you about Houdini sometime."

"That would be great, Rabbi."

OUTSIDE THE THEATER

Renaldo and Jared stood on the sidewalk scanning the faces of the crowd leaving the building. Streetlamps and the marquee sign over the theater lit the area. The artificial light spread its rays across the cobblestone sidewalk and onto the cracked cement of the street. The night was cool for Miami, and Renaldo pulled his sport jacket tighter around him. People crossed the road in packs, hailing cabs and climbing into cars that waited by the curb.

"Where is he?" Jared asked. "He should have come out by now."

Renaldo watched an elderly couple get into a car. "Patience, Jared. One must always be patient, and don't look so agitated. We don't want to call attention to ourselves."

"It's hard not to be agitated when what you told me isn't happening."

"I thought for sure he'd be picked up in front of the theater. That's what my inside source connected to the magician said would happen."

Jared's gaze darted left and right. "Already things are starting to go wrong."

"Maybe he stayed to talk to people after the show. A minor setback. Keep your head and we'll get him inside the theater."

"Inside? Are you crazy? We'd never escape. We must rethink our plan and try again later. It's too dangerous now."

"Cousin, I am the expert."

"But I've got my instincts. This is wrong. We're bound to fail."

"We do it tonight." Renaldo's words came out angry and clipped. He glared at Jared and then stepped into the warmer theater. Renaldo scanned the faces of the few who remained in the lobby. None were the magician. He pushed open the door and walked down the center aisle toward the stage. Jared slowly followed.

A stagehand picked up a few programs on the floor that had

been left behind. He straightened and stared at Renaldo and Jared as they moved up the aisle. "The show's over. I'm afraid you'll have to leave the theater."

Jared touched his sport jacket, feeling the holstered gun underneath.

Renaldo shook his head slightly at Jared and then smiled at the stagehand. "I'm sorry, but I seem to have lost my wallet. It must have fallen out of my pants during that wonderful performance. The magician was great, was he not? Could I check where I was sitting? I had it during intermission so that is the only place it could be."

The stagehand followed them. "Sure. Let me help you look. What seats were you in?"

Renaldo walked quickly to get away. "No. I'm fine. I'm sure you have other things to do."

He noticed the magician deep in the wings talking to another man. A beautiful Spanish woman was nearby. He glanced around the theater, which was empty except for the stagehand behind him and a few people clearing the stage of props. A shot from this distance might miss its mark. They must not fail. He'd given his word. Not to succeed would be unthinkable. He sprinted toward the stairs leading up to the stage.

"Stop!" the stagehand yelled. "You can't go up there."

Weiss and Stanford looked toward the screaming.

Renaldo reached the top step, snapped his gun from the leather holster, and focused on his target.

In that instant, Rabbi Weiss realized the object in the man's hand glistening in the overhead lights was a gun.

Renaldo's arm straightened, but the stagehand grabbed him from behind. Renaldo drove his elbow hard into the man's kidneys, knocking him backward.

Weiss shoved Stanford back into the curtain. The magician's feet tangled in the fabric and he fell to his knees, his eyes showing confusion, and the books he carried flew to the floor. Weiss moved forward, pushing Solea out of the way.

Renaldo turned on his heels, searching for the magician.

A bullet ricocheted off the cement wall behind Weiss. Then a second shot was fired wildly.

Weiss dove behind a big metal case just as a bullet struck him in the heart.

Several people scurried from behind the stage, confusion evident on their faces. They scattered in different directions when what was happening became evident; some went back behind the stage while others hit the floor.

Renaldo spotted Jared racing up the aisle and toward the lobby. *Coward,* he wanted to scream.

Renaldo, his anger rising, swiveled with the gun. He needed to make sure the magician was dead. He heard shouts from behind him. Several people had come in from the lobby at the sound of the shots. He was losing control of the situation and realized that without Jared he had no backup. He had to assume the shot to the heart had killed his target.

Keeping his weapon drawn, he backed down the stairs. Out of the corner of his eye, he saw the magician stand. *Impossible,* he thought. Could the stories about him being immortal be true? A few people came through the exit several feet away and Renaldo thought only of escape. He ran up the aisle and out the door.

Rabbi Weiss walked from behind the metal case, reached out his hand, and helped the young magician to his feet. Stanford's eyes focused on the bullet burn hole, still smoldering on Weiss's jacket. But the man was alive. *Is he a God? Or Superman?* he thought. He didn't even appear to be shaken.

"You're all right, Rabbi," Stanford said, pointing to the hole in his jacket, the astonishment showing on his face.

Weiss looked down, then reached inside his jacket, pulled a prayer book out of his pocket, and opened it. The bullet was embedded in the book. A metal key Weiss kept in the back of the book had stopped it from penetrating his heart.

"I guess the Siddur saved my life."

"You're a lucky man, Rabbi," Stanford said.

Weiss smiled, fingered the bullet hole, then slipped the Siddur back inside his jacket. "I've always felt God looked after me." He turned to a stagehand standing nearby. "Call the police. Those men were imbeciles. How could they possibly think they could get away with this?"

Stanford wiped dirt off his shirt, walked to Solea, and wrapped his arms around her. "Are you all right, honey?"

"Yes," she said, her voice steady, her eyes locked on the Rabbi's. "Is Miami always this dangerous?"

"No. It's usually a very safe place."

Stanford picked the two books off the floor. "I'm not used to having people take shots at me after my show. When I first spotted the guy with the gun I thought he was an Elvis impersonator."

"He was very distinctive looking. The police shouldn't have much trouble finding him. I didn't get a good look at the second gunman, did you?"

Stanford shook his head. "The whole scene was surrealistic. It was like it happened in slow motion. Any idea what the attack was all about?"

Weiss touched his beard. "Unfortunately, I think I do."

Stanford walked away from Solea, leaned close to Weiss, and lowered his voice. "Those men were after you, weren't they?"

Weiss glanced over his shoulder to be sure no one was listening. "It was just a random attack by two crazy men."

Stanford pointed to the hole in the Rabbi's jacket and shook his head. "The gunman wanted to kill you. He had a clear shot at me, but didn't take it. It would take a fool not to realize you were the target, and I'm not a fool. You have enemies, Rabbi. Why?"

"I'm afraid it's a long story that goes back many years."

"Do you have secrets?"

"Everyone has secrets. I had hoped this one would stay with me until I died a natural death."

"Well, it seemed like those two were trying to make sure your demise was a lot quicker than you planned. I hope the cops catch them before they try again."

Weiss stood straighter, a grim, determined look on his face. Then he mumbled, "The police can't be told the truth. No, that won't work."

"What are you talking about? Don't you want them to be caught?"

"It's bigger than those two men."

"Rabbi, I have no idea what you mean, but if you'd like to talk about it sometime I'm willing to listen. Maybe I can help."

Weiss studied the young magician for several seconds. "You might be able to at that. When you return the books to me, I might have quite a story to tell you. Before that I have some decisions to make."

TEMPLE MENORAH, 75 STREET – MIAMI BEACH

An occasional car whisked along the boulevard, but at two a.m., it was mostly cabs. A light rain fell and the air smelled of salt and copper. The streetlights reflected on the damp sidewalk and beyond to the front door of Rabbi Weiss's temple. The man had entered a few minutes before.

Renaldo and Jared raced from the side of the building, crossed the street, and hid in the shadows of a doorway. Renaldo was still shaken that the magician had survived the attack at the theater. Hadn't he seen the bullet penetrate his heart? Maybe his eyes had played a trick on him. No man could have survived that wound.

Jared stared at the temple as minutes passed. "It didn't work. Everything we tried tonight fell apart. Let's get out of here. Maybe we should leave Miami before word of our failure gets out. I hear the west coast is nice for our line of work."

"Relax, Jared. We're not leaving Miami. Things are good here. You are too impatient. It takes a while for the fuse to ignite. I've done this type of work before. You will see. Our boss will be very happy with our ingenuity. If there's one thing I've learned over the years, it's to always have a backup plan. I'd hoped not to use the explosives, but now I'm glad I brought them."

"I told you your idea of killing the magician at the theater wouldn't work. You should have listened to me. We almost got killed."

Renaldo's eyebrows shot up a notch. "Only because of you. We might have succeeded if you hadn't deserted me. Your job was to make sure no one stopped me, but you ran off like a coward."

Jared's face reddened. "Since when can't you take care of an overweight stagehand? I made sure no one came in from the lobby. If I felt you were in any danger, I would have helped. You know you can count on me."

Renaldo studied the young man. "I thought I knew you, Cousin. Maybe I will have to reconsider whether we do any jobs together in the future."

There was a muffled roar—orange light illuminated the neighborhood and then shards of metal, glass, and brick flew onto the road. A second explosion shook the area. It was a ferocious sound—one so close Renaldo felt the breath sucked out of him. The two men crouched low and held their arms up for protection from the heat.

Renaldo straightened, smiled, and stared at the flames shooting from the temple. "The man is dead. There is no way he could have survived that explosion. Our boss may want to give us a raise because of our creativity. I'm sure he'll have many more jobs for us." He jabbed a finger at Jared. "I'll believe what you say about abandoning me this one time, Jared. Any future problems and you will know what pure terror is when you have to deal with me."

Renaldo and Jared ran up the street, away from the temple, just as sirens sounded in the distance.

4
Houdini Lives! And Appears On My TV Show

Rabbi Weiss and Jackie Gleason were seated at a back table in Wolfie's Deli. A curtain separated them from the main room and the two men talked quietly so as not to be overheard. They'd finished lunch. Gleason had feasted on an overstuffed corned beef sandwich while Weiss had sipped from a bowl of vegetable soup. The Rabbi had asked for the meeting with Gleason. The comedian wondered why but knew better than to ask. Weiss would tell him when he was ready.

Gleason pushed the empty plate away. "Wolfie's has the best food. There's nothing like a light lunch to get you through the day."

Weiss grinned. "You call that a light lunch?"

Gleason patted his stomach. "For a growing guy like me it is." He pointed to the Rabbi's empty bowl. "You hardly ate. It's no wonder you're in such great shape. You have the same physique you had forty years ago."

"Working out and staying fit is a habit to me. For so many years I needed to be in the best condition possible. It's what people expected."

"We've known each other for a long time, Houdini, and you still won't tell me the secrets of your great escapes. How about just one?"

Weiss put his finger to his lips. "Please keep your voice down. How many times have I asked you to call me Rabbi Weiss?

29

Especially now. I feel fortunate to be sitting with you today after the attempts on my life. The temple exploded just minutes after I left. If I'd stayed any longer I would have been killed."

Gleason frowned and fidgeted in his seat. "Thank God you got out, but it's still a tragedy that the building was destroyed and so many historical documents were lost. Was everything burned?"

"We managed to save a few things, and I promise you that we will rebuild."

"It's started again, hasn't it?"

The Rabbi nodded. "There's no question I was the target."

Gleason waved his hand toward the room. "Shouldn't you be more careful about being out in public?"

"Weiss glanced at the curtain that shrouded them. "There are people looking out for me."

"Still," Gleason said, "if someone tried to kill me I'd stay away from crowded places."

Weiss shrugged. "One cannot live life in fear. If someone is intent on killing me they'll find me no matter where I am."

"Do the police have any suspects?"

"Not yet, but they do have excellent descriptions. What they haven't been able to figure out is a motive."

"The newspapers are playing this story up big. Front-page everyday. The cops are under a lot of pressure to make an arrest. If those two men are still in Miami it won't be long until they're captured."

"If they're smart they'll be far away from here by now."

Gleason gave Weiss a long stare. "The accounts of the shooting you've given to the press have been sketchy. You've refused all interviews, and my sources with the police tell me you've given them little to go on. Why aren't you telling the cops all you know? Wouldn't that help catch the men?"

"Being totally honest right now could cost me my life. I must pick the right time to reveal all, but I admit the shooting at the theater has shaken me badly. I looked directly into the killer's eyes as he fumbled to get his gun out of his holster. The question is why would they decide to kill me after all this time?"

"They?" Gleason asked.

Weiss waved the question off. "I've been hiding out in Miami for almost forty years. I thought I was safe."

"You've made mention of past attempts on your life, but

never told me your suspicions about who was behind it. I have a lot of connections across the country. I might be able to track the people down."

Weiss smiled. "Now you're a detective? No, this is something I must handle by myself. If I could just figure out how I was uncovered, that might give me a clue as to why they're coming after me again." He hesitated. "Maybe word leaked out that you were trying to convince me to appear on your Halloween Magic Show and that's how they found me."

"Hey, I was pretty evasive on The Larry King Show the other night. You hadn't agreed to appear, but I was confident I could convince you. I don't think anyone figured out you were alive from what I said on that broadcast."

"I totally agree, but one of your assistants might have leaked it."

"Impossible. There are only a few of my men who know your real identity, and I can vouch for them. They wouldn't betray you."

"People will do many things for a price."

"Not my people."

"No, but others might. Maybe one of your men spoke to someone in all innocence. All I know is the temple explosion and the shooting were attempts to kill me, and this time innocent people could have been hurt. I've remained silent for too long. I must put a stop to this madness. It's just a question of how."

Gleason shook his head slowly. "I still find it hard to believe you were poisoned forty years ago just before you performed the Water Torture Cell Escape. It all seems so bizarre. You were one of the most famous people in the world. Surely, whoever tried to do this knew they'd be caught."

"But they weren't, were they? Desperate people will take chances. If there's one thing I'm sure of it's that forty years ago someone wanted to silence me. And they succeeded in some ways. Bess had been poisoned just a few weeks before and almost died. That's why we decided to fake my death and get away. I could have fought them, but they knew my wife was my weakness. Family has always been more important to me than anything else."

"How did you manage to fake your death?"

"That's one thing I'll never talk about. I'll take that secret to the grave."

"You were a well known entertainer and a hero to millions. It's just hard for me to comprehend someone so intent on killing you."

"Jackie, we've been friends for many years, and I trust you implicitly, but this is something I can't share with you. The knowledge would be dangerous. All I know is I must figure out a way to stop them, and I think I know how to do it. I just hope I'm right."

"You're risking your life by playing this game, Rabbi. You should be talking to the police and letting the professionals handle it."

Weiss shook his head. "The attempts on my life run much deeper than the two men at the theater. Sure, they may be arrested, but there are others ready to take their place. This calls for drastic action, which is why I needed to meet with you."

Gleason took a gulp from his coffee mug and wiped his mouth with a napkin. "I wondered when you'd get to that. What's on your mind?"

"Can I assume that even with everything that's happened you still want me to appear on your Halloween special on magic?"

Gleason leaned forward. "Are you kidding? Have I finally convinced you? Think of the rating bonanza. Houdini lives and appears on my show forty years after his assumed death. No one could top that. The last time we talked, you weren't sure. What changed your mind?"

"The attempt on my life made me question my own mortality and the bombing of the temple angered me. I may not have much longer to live." Weiss smiled to relieve the seriousness of his statement. "Besides, show business has always been in my blood. Seeing a young magician perform the other night brought those emotions back to me. It's time I reappeared."

"Is that definite? You won't change your mind?"

"I will appear on two conditions. First, no one must know I am scheduled to be on your show. You can hint that something spectacular will happen concerning Houdini, as you've already done, but under no circumstances are you to mention that I will appear."

"You're taking some of the fun out of this."

"It would be too dangerous otherwise. Killing me on live television would be too tempting to the men intent on doing it.

Members of your audience could be hurt. I won't go on otherwise."

Gleason forced a smile; his expression indicated he wasn't happy. "What's your second condition?"

"I want to be able to talk freely to the millions that watch that night. You're not to ask me what I'm going to say or try to censor me in any way. Do you accept my two conditions?"

"If I do, then you'll guarantee to be on my show?"

"Only my death would stop me."

"Don't even joke about that, Rabbi."

"Then you agree?"

"If that's the only way I can book you, then so be it. I'll play up the surprise angle, but I won't say you'll be appearing on my show. Will you perform tricks for my audience? Can I at least count on that?"

"I am an old man now, but I may be able to recreate some of my former illusions. I've kept many of my locks and handcuffs hidden away at my home. Some nights when I'm in my study alone, I still practice the old tricks. It's not the same without an audience. It would be great to recreate some magic in front of people again."

Gleason rose and held out his hand. What he really wanted to do was hug the Rabbi. "This will be an event people will always remember. Forget the Beatles and Elvis on the Sullivan show. It'll be Houdini on the Gleason show that will stick. When my viewers see you performing they won't believe their eyes."

Weiss got to his feet and shook Gleason's hand. "The real trick will be to survive until Halloween night."

5

STANFORD AND SOLEA ARGUE

L arry King pulled the microphone closer. Frank Sinatra, seated a few inches away, adjusted his tie. The producer pointed a finger at them.

"Welcome back to the Larry King Show. Our guest tonight is Frank Sinatra. Frank, you've got a new album out, 'Strangers in the Night', which is just incredible."

"That's why I like doing this show, Larry. You always know the right thing to say. Yeah, it is a good one and later this year my label is putting out 'Sinatra at the Sands', which is a live concert recording. They tell me I still sound pretty good."

"Better than ever, Frank. Let me ask you something that seems to be on everyone's mind here in Miami. Your pal, Gleason, was here the other night. He's doing a Halloween special on magicians. He's got something unusual planned that has to do with Harry Houdini. Gleason, a man who usually can't keep his mouth shut, was secretive about what's going on. Have you heard anything?"

Sinatra laughed. "You mean like is he going to bring the magician back from the dead? I don't think even Gleason could do that."

"Why do you think the public is still fascinated by Houdini?"

"Because he was a giant. Man, I'd love to pull off some of the publicity exploits he did. Anytime he visited a new town, he'd perform some kind of stunt. He'd have the cops lock him in a cell and within minutes, he'd break out or have them handcuff him and seconds later give the cuffs back. A few times he'd be put in a strait jacket and be suspended upside down over a busy street. I even read where he was handcuffed and pushed through a hole in an ice-covered river. A few minutes later, he bobbed though the hole and put the cuffs on the ice. Think of the mind of the person who could come up with these tricks. He was a master showman who knew how to keep crowds talking, but let's face it, he's been dead for forty years. Besides, the guy didn't drink. I never trust a guy who doesn't drink."

"Figuring out how to break out of a jail cell would be a good trick for you to learn."

Sinatra smiled. "That's low, Larry, even for you. The point is, Houdini would do anything to call attention to himself. My buddy Gleason's the same way. I don't know what Jackie has planned, but everybody's talking about it. That's a tribute to Houdini. The guy is still a legend even after all this time. I hope to have the same kind of respect when I'm gone."

"I have a feeling you will, Frank. You're appearing in the area. Why don't you tell the audience where they can see you?"

"I'm doing a gig at the Fontainebleau with my pal, Sammy Davis Jr., right through Friday, and it's going to be a blast. Going to do all my hits and have a few surprises. When Sammy and I get together, it's always like one big party. I'm inviting your audience to come see my show. Even Harry Houdini, if he happens to be listening in."

King laughed. "He's probably getting ready for his Gleason appearance."

"Well, I know I'll be watching. I've got a feeling that whatever happens will be amazing."

DIPLOMAT HOTEL – MIAMI BEACH

Stanford sat in an ornate cherry wood chair in front of a walnut desk with the books on Houdini open in front of him. A breeze wafted in through the open window and rustled the curtains. In the corner, next to the bureau, his suitcase rested on the floor, his clothes in a pile on top of it. The room smelled of salt water and sex. This wasn't a four-star hotel, but at least Weiss had put them up in a place fancier than some of the others he'd stayed in over the years. Someday he'd stay only in lavish rooms.

He'd skimmed through the books focusing on the wide variety of tricks Houdini performed. The man was truly amazing, and reading about him again inspired Stanford to become even better.

He'd spent a lot of time reading the specifics of each illusion, and he pictured the great man on stage going through his routine. He felt honored to know how some of them were done.

He turned a page and studied one of the pictures of Houdini as a young magician. He thought back to his own early days as a teenager. He'd built a wooden theater, complete with a stage and a marquee in his back yard, and painted "Stanford's Magic Show" in bold black letters on it. The rush of performing, even then, thrilled him, and the shows he put on became his life. His parents called him obsessive and over confident, but the cockiness he showed onstage even now hid the doubts he sometimes felt. Sure, he wanted to be successful, but so did many others. Was he that much better than other magicians?

He flipped a few more pages and watched the transformation of Houdini as he became older. Even in his later years, he had remained in remarkable shape. The regime and hard work that must have gone into keeping him in top form was astounding. He knew that with the same dedication he'd be doing magic for years to come.

He studied Houdini's face; the shape of his eyes, the slant to his nose, and then lips. That was when it struck him.

"Holy shit," he muttered. "Holy shit."

Was it the eyes? The posture? The way he held his hands? Stanford examined the picture closer and realized the magician had an amazing resemblance to Rabbi Weiss.

He thought back to the night he'd met Weiss. The Rabbi had come backstage and they'd talked about magic. Weiss had talked enthusiastically about many of the old timers, and it quickly became obvious that he deeply admired Houdini. Stanford thought at the time that the old man knew an awful lot about illusions himself.

He scrutinized the idea, forming in his mind and made every attempt to rule it out. It was impossible. Or was it? He remembered reading the rumors that Houdini had faked his death in 1926.

He scrunched his eyes and moved closer to a photo taken at one of Houdini's last performances. He covered the bottom of the magician's face with his hand and tried to picture him with a beard and older, with wrinkles. The similarities were uncanny. The age would be right, as would the height.

He put his head back and closed his eyes, remembering what he'd read about Houdini's last few months. There had been attempts on his life and on the life of his wife, Bess. These attempts were said to have been made by psychics intent on silencing him for revealing their secrets in his stage act. The magician had become obsessed with this, and many psychics had been humiliated. Could Houdini have performed the ultimate illusion by disappearing for forty years? This would have been the greatest trick ever done.

He flashed back to the attempt on the Rabbi's life after the fundraiser. Stanford was convinced the Rabbi knew the reason someone had tried to kill him. Yet he'd been reluctant to talk to the police. Could psychics be trying to kill him again? That wouldn't make sense. Weiss was no threat to them.

He smiled. How many knew that Houdini's real name was Ehrich Weiss? Taking his own name would be just like the magician. His confidence and arrogance made him feel he could get away with anything.

He studied a few more pictures and became more convinced. How could no one else have seen this? He remembered one of his early lessons in magic—people see only what they expect to see. There were too many coincidences for it not to be true. He'd confront the Rabbi and make him tell the truth. He felt he was about to make one of the greatest discoveries of his young life, and he knew exactly how to take advantage of it.

If he were right, meeting Rabbi Weiss would be the event that would give him an edge over all other magicians. Imagine, getting to talk to the real Houdini.

He refocused on the book and was so engrossed that he was unaware that Solea had come back from her walk on the beach. She slipped in silently and stood over him, dressed in a colorful flowered blouse and tight fitting black slacks.

She walked behind him, looked over the top of the chair, then put her hands on his shoulders and began to knead gently. "You're very tense."

Stanford turned a page. He didn't want to tell her what he was thinking until Weiss admitted the truth. "I've got a lot on my mind. This book is amazing."

Solea rubbed harder. "You have to learn to relax. I know how important your career is to you, but isn't there something you'd rather do? Maybe something I can do to make you feel better?"

Stanford smiled and felt a familiar tingle pass through his body. "Again? My God, you're insatiable." He put the book on the table, got up, and put his arms around Solea, pulling her into him tightly. "You're the best thing that ever happened to me. How'd I get so lucky?"

Solea looked into his eyes. "You were smart enough to hire me as your assistant. Out of all the gorgeous women on the beach that wanted the job you selected me."

"You were the most beautiful. How could I resist?"

He pushed her hair behind her ear. He'd known her only a short time, and her mood swings startled him. At times, she was loving and caring. But often she seemed cold and withdrawn, as if she had serious matters on her mind. When he'd ask about it, she'd say nothing was wrong and it was his imagination. But, he knew better. He was a student of human nature. As a magician, he had to be. Solea was holding something back. He had no idea what it was, but he hoped someday she'd trust him enough to reveal it.

What did he know about her anyway? She'd mentioned an uncle in Miami, but had talked little about her life in Barcelona. She had said that while in Spain she'd waitressed in a relative's restaurant, but aside from that, he knew nothing of her family and friends.

He put his finger under her chin, tilted her head up, and kissed her lightly on the lips.

Solea pulled back gently. "What's wrong? You seem preoccupied."

"No. Everything's fine."

A frown crossed her face. "Is it me? Are you having second thoughts about hiring me?"

"Of course not. How could you even think that?"

Solea's shoulders slumped and she turned away. The last thing he wanted was to hurt her. Maybe the best thing to do would be to admit what he'd learned and make her see the importance of his discovery. He knew it would be difficult to keep this secret from her. Besides, he was bursting to tell someone.

"I've got to show you something." Picking up the book, he opened it and pointed to a picture. "Can you see it?"

Solea studied Stanford's face for a moment and then looked at the book. "See what?"

"Don't you know who Rabbi Weiss is?"

"Sure. He's a cool old man who likes doing nice things for kids."

"No, Solea. He's Harry Houdini."

Solea stood straighter, a slight smile formed on her face. "What have you been smoking? Houdini died long ago."

Stanford tapped the picture with his finger. "That's what he wants people to think, but there have always been rumors that he survived and his disappearance was his ultimate trick. I'm convinced Weiss is Houdini. Someone found out the truth and tried to kill him."

"Hold it. Think about what you're saying. It's ridiculous. The attempt on his life was done by two crazy men. No one will know why until they're captured, but it has nothing to do with Houdini."

"I think it does and that Rabbi Weiss has been hiding out for forty years. There were attempts on his life in 1926. Now someone's come after him again."

Solea sat on the arm of the chair. "That makes no sense at all. It's impossible."

Stanford turned to another page and held the book toward Solea. "Look. Study his face. Picture him older and with a beard. The resemblance is uncanny. He'd be the right age. That would explain his interest in magic and why he gave me the books."

"Maybe magic excites him as much as it does you. Did you think of that?"

"You should have seen his eyes sparkle when he talked of Houdini. That's because he was talking about himself. Do you know what Houdini's real name was?"

Solea shook her head, the look of disbelief still on her face.

"Ehrich Weiss."

"Well, that settles it," Solea said. "Houdini wouldn't take his real name if he were trying to hide out."

"No, it would be right in character for Houdini. The man had a gigantic ego. He felt he could accomplish anything. Very often he wore a disguise, went out in public, and no one recognized him. Taking the family name would be a way to honor his mother and father, whom he respected deeply. Besides, Weiss is a common name and with people believing Houdini dead, no one would be looking for him. It's the type of stunt he loved."

"Everything you've mentioned so far could be a coincidence. It doesn't prove anything."

"There is one way I can be one hundred percent certain. Even you wouldn't be able to doubt it. There's always been a rumor about Houdini. Something that, if Weiss has it, will prove I'm right. When I return the books I will examine him closely."

"I have no idea what you're talking about. Why are you being so mysterious?"

"I read about it while I was doing research on magic. Houdini had a secret. Something he'd do when he was in a situation even he couldn't get out of. There were times he did things so miraculous that this secret would be the only logical explanation. I'd tell you, my love, but you know how we magicians are reluctant to reveal our secrets. It would spoil the illusion. Besides, I may decide to use this device myself someday."

"If you're right, and I'm not certain you are, wouldn't it be dangerous for Rabbi Weiss to reveal his identity to you, especially if someone is trying to kill him? He barely knows you."

"He gave me these books for a reason. I think he was reaching out to me. After the shooting, I asked him if he had any idea why it happened. He told me it was a long story that went back many years. He said when I returned the books he might tell me. I think he's going to reveal his true identity to me. Why else would he say that?"

"There could be many logical reasons. Sometimes your imagination is too vivid."

"Not in this case. When I prove he's Houdini I'm going to use that knowledge to further my career."

"Come on. Even if Weiss were Houdini what benefit would that be to you?"

Stanford's eyes widened. "Are you kidding? Imagine the publicity I'd get if I could say I actually talked to Houdini forty years after his death and he told me his secrets. People would flock to see Houdini's protégé. I would become the new Houdini."

"People would just say you were crazy."

"All the better. Think of the crowds that would want to see a crazy man."

Solea pushed back a lock of hair, a pensive look on her face. "Sometimes your ambition frightens me."

"I'm doing this for us, Solea. To make our life better. Believe me, I'd never do anything to harm what we have. I think Houdini's concerned about the attempts on his life and feels I can help."

"How could you help?"

"I don't know. Possibly he'll tell me when I see him."

Solea shook her head. "Even if Weiss is Houdini, why would he tell you the secrets of his magic? You've told me many times how magicians are reluctant to reveal the truth behind their illusions. And Houdini isn't just any magician. He's the best."

Stanford jabbed a finger at her. "This is different. Houdini would love this. No one pulled more publicity stunts to further his career than he did. Weiss told me he studied the craft a little. Yeah, right. To think I was talking to Houdini himself and didn't know it. When I return his books, I'll find out the truth. He's too old to perform, but he could relive his illusions through me. It's my job to convince him to do it, and you know how persuasive I can be."

"You're really certain of this, aren't you?"

"Yeah, I am and soon you will be, too."

"I don't like this at all. What if the men who tried to kill Houdini come after you?"

"Solea, you've been watching too many American movies. Why would anyone want to kill a young magician like me?"

"Maybe for the same reason they want Houdini dead. Maybe he has secrets the killers are afraid he will reveal. What if they think he told you, and you become a threat to them?"

"I'll talk to Houdini and find out why these men are after him. But there's one thing I want from him more than anything else." He turned a few pages in the book and pointed. "I need for Houdini to teach me his most masterful illusion, the famous Water Torture Cell Escape. It's the trick people think killed him. I'll perform it live on television. Millions will want to watch his protégée try the most famous illusion of all time. Once that happens, we'll be on our way. I'll be booked on the top television shows and in the best theaters. Even Gleason and Sullivan will fight to have me on. I'll be able to command any price. Think of what we can do with that money."

"I don't care about money. I want you alive. Men have died trying to perform that stunt."

"Ah. But others have not had the help of Houdini. With his guidance, I couldn't fail. I'll do it and then move beyond him. My goal is to become greater than Houdini. There'll be no stopping me."

"Sometimes I think you love the spotlight more than you love me."

"That's not fair. You're not listening. I'm doing this for us. I knew the right woman would come along for me sometime, and you're that woman. We have a great life ahead of us. Nothing is going to spoil that, and nothing is going to happen to me. I absolutely guarantee it."

"There's more to life than magic. I need your attention, too."

"And you'll get it. Do you have any idea how exciting this is for me? To get to talk to the real Houdini about magic?"

"What if he won't help you? What if he refuses to admit who he is? What will you do then?"

"I'll perform the trick anyway." He pounded his chest. "I won't let his refusal stop me." He turned to Solea, rubbed her cheek, and then kissed her lightly on the lips. "What was that you said about doing something to make me feel better?"

She smiled seductively. "Again?"

6

KIRK, THIS IS UNACCEPTABLE

Renaldo and Jared lowered their heads. The man in front of them was in his late fifties, ruggedly good looking with a shock of gray hair. He was dressed in a white knit shirt and gray slacks. Seated behind the dark, oak wood desk, surrounded by built-in bookcases, the man's body was rigid. Visible out a window behind him, the surf pounded against giant rocks. Chopin played softly through speakers in the background.

Renaldo looked up at him. "Mr. Kirk, there were unexpected developments. Surely you . . ."

Kirk glared at them—Renaldo, with his shiny suit, big pads under the shoulders, and pointed toed shoes, and Jared, the more casual of the two with his black shirt and pants. Both men were nervous, and they had a right to be.

Kirk slammed his fist on the desk, his face red with anger. He was used to giving orders and having them obeyed. "You've failed. This is totally unacceptable. I don't want to hear excuses."

"But . . ." Renaldo stammered.

Kirk flicked his hand. "You promised me that Houdini would be eliminated. I trusted you and you've betrayed that trust. And the fucking stupidity of blowing up the temple is beyond belief. You've read what he's saying in the papers. He's angry, and there's no telling what an infuriated man will do. Especially one as crazy as Houdini."

Renaldo glanced at Jared, who kept his eyes focused on the floor. "He didn't act as expected. He stayed in the theater and

45

talked to the young magician. How could we have known? Jared and I did everything possible. Didn't we, Jared?"

Jared nodded.

Kirk glared at him. "Do you have any idea what your failure means?"

Jared didn't respond.

"Maybe if you'd explained more about the mission," Renaldo said.

"Why? You would have tried harder? Our phone conversations were sufficient. If you had questions you should have asked. I told you we were never to meet. That nothing was to connect us. The only reason I demanded to see you today was because of your failure."

"We came so close, Mr. Kirk," Renaldo said. "I was on the stage with the magician and had a clear shot but was attacked from behind." He decided not to mention the bullet he'd witnessed penetrating the magician's heart. He didn't want Kirk to doubt his sanity.

"What was your partner doing all this time?"

"He was right with me. No one could have gotten to Houdini under those circumstances. When he went into the temple, the lights went out. We thought he stayed inside."

Kirk swept his hand toward the men. "You two are fucking imbeciles. Of course the lights went out. He was going home and left through the back door, as he always does. Had you done any surveillance on the man you would have known he didn't live in the temple. Or didn't you think you had to do any advance planning? That Houdini would stand still and allow himself to be killed. You two are nothing but clowns. You blew up an empty building and brought the wrath of the community upon us. The cops won't stop until they track you down."

Renaldo touched his sideburn. "We have an underground network of people that will hide us."

"Idiots." Spittle flew from Kirk's mouth. "The only important thing is the result, and you produced nothing." He pounded on the table. "Nothing. You should have planned for all contingencies. Now Houdini will be on guard more than before. How could you be so fucking incompetent?"

Renaldo looked at Jared as if expecting him to speak. When he didn't, he said, "We will find out where he is going to be tonight and take him out. There will be no mistakes. I guarantee it on my mother's grave. We will not fail this time."

Kirk shook his head angrily. "No way. You've had your chance. You came highly recommended to me by the Cuban underground. You wouldn't fail they told me. You were the best. But you did fail, didn't you. You're too fucking incompetent to allow to have another go at Houdini."

Jared looked up. "We're very sorry, Mr. Kirk."

"Oh, you can speak. I was beginning to think you were a mute. Sorry doesn't cut it with me. Were you frightened by the rumors that said Houdini couldn't be killed? Did you cower like a woman at the thought of him?"

Renaldo stood straighter, but his thoughts flickered back to the magician's survival of the attack. "Of course not, Mr. Kirk. We fear no man."

"Houdini is like no one else. I can't believe how you blundered."

"Give us one more chance, Mr. Kirk. Please," Jared said.

Kirk blew air out of his nose. "*Please, Mr. Kirk. Give us one more chance.* You two are pathetic. I will never give you another chance." He opened the desk drawer and put his hand inside. "There is one other thing I do need from you, however."

Renaldo smiled and glanced at Jared. "Anything. Jared and I will do whatever it takes to make up for this."

"Anything is right. You will give me your lives." Kirk pulled a .45 out of the desk and pointed it at Renaldo.

Renaldo's face whitened and he held up his hands. "Mr. Kirk, please. We'll give you back the money you paid us and take out Houdini for free. We are all rational men here."

"Rational?" Kirk shook his head. "A man cannot be rational if he is surrounded by imperfection."

"But, I explained. It wasn't our fault."

"Save your breath." Kirk cocked the hammer of the gun. "The cops will pick you up and to save your lives you'll lead them right to me."

"Never." Renaldo backed up a step. "We are men of honor. We would never betray you."

The two men locked eyes.

"By failure you signed your own death warrant."

"You're crazy," Renaldo said, his gaze darting right and left looking for a way to escape.

Jared raced toward the door.

Kirk pulled the trigger. One shot, a second, and then a third. Renaldo clutched his throat; a low gurgling sound came from his mouth. Then he slumped to the floor. Jared fell a few feet away.

Kirk laughed, not one of joy but more like a demented killer. "One is not crazy if he seeks justice for a good cause."

A shadowy figure came out from an adjoining room. Jose Ramirez had watched the killing through a crack in the door. The Cuban was forty-seven but looked younger. His jet-black hair was slicked back, and he had a squat, powerful body. Dressed in a dark business suit he looked more like an accountant than a cold-blooded killer.

He stepped around the bodies, looking at them in disdain. "These bunglers deserved to die. You made a mistake by hiring them. I hope in the future you will let me handle things like this for you." He pointed toward Renaldo and Jared. "I will see that their bodies are disposed of."

Kirk placed the gun on top of the desk. "No. I screwed up. I know just the place to get rid of them. There will be no other mistakes when it comes to Houdini. I promise that on my father's grave."

"See that there isn't. We don't want anything to disrupt our plans."

"Nothing will do that. We've come too far for that."

Kirk walked to a dark, mahogany cabinet and opened it. He took out a bottle of brandy and two crystal snifters. Uncorking the bottle he filled two glasses and handed one to Jose.

Kirk hoisted his glass. "To the success of our mission."

They clinked glasses and each took a sip.

"This is wonderful brandy, Anthony. I hope our future is as sweet."

"It will be. In two years I will be in the White House."

Jose wiped his mustache with the sleeve of his jacket. "Have you been in spiritual contact with your father again?"

"I have. My father, the greatest psychic of all time, has predicted my success. Houdini destroyed this incredible man with his lies. I watched him die a penniless and broken man. At his graveside I vowed revenge."

Jose sighed. "Yes. Yes. You've told me your story many times. I care about none of that. My fear is that Houdini will start speaking out when he hears of our plans and realizes who your father was. He had a vendetta against your family and that could cost us votes, if not the election. We've put a lot of money and resources behind you. Whatever you've wanted, we've supplied. We don't need any controversy surrounding the next president."

"And none will occur once the magician is dead. I promise you that. You have assisted me, but I also helped you. Didn't I guide you through the Bay of Pigs invasion? And when it was decided that John Kennedy had to be eliminated, who advised you on the assassination? You yourself said it couldn't have been done without me. I've supported your cause and the Cuban people for years."

Jose put his hand on Kirk's shoulder. "That you have, my friend. You are considered a great man in Florida. An ambitious businessman and a natural leader. As CEO of Divi Rum, you proved that a person could turn a few thousand dollars into millions. Your fame is now spreading to other states, as we get ready for the next election. People are looking for a true visionary and are already clamoring for you to run for president thanks to our carefully orchestrated campaign. There is no office not for sale in America. Including the highest prize."

"Ah, but the true reward is having someone in the White House who will put our dreams into effect. We will bring an end to democracy in America."

"But LBJ will have to be dealt with first."

"Johnson is no threat. The Vietnam War will destroy any chance he has of getting elected, especially when I announce I have a secret plan to end the war. Only the Cuban Underground will know that it's to take our troops out and let Vietnam fall. Communism will spread across the Pacific, and when it reaches the west coast of the United States we will welcome it. Americans are fat and complacent. By the time they realize what's happening, it will be too late. That will be the end of their freedoms." He jabbed his chest. "I will decide what is good for America. I've already compiled a list of people I will have jailed."

"And we must not let a madman like Houdini interfere with that goal. He is so well known people will listen. We can't afford to have the media take a careful look into your past. They may uncover your connection to us, and that would be the end of careful years of planning." Jose took another sip of brandy.

"Tell me how you intend to have Houdini killed."

Kirk waved his hand. "You've no need to know the details. The important thing is that this time nothing will go wrong. That's an ironclad guarantee. My niece, Solea, has been very helpful to us. I made sure she got a job as an assistant to a young magician who knows Houdini. Solea is very ambitious and knows the importance of family. She will feed us information. I have big plans for her and intend to take her with us to the White House. She will be very beneficial to our cause."

"How do we know Solea can be trusted?"

"She wouldn't dare be disloyal to her uncle. If I felt she was, then I would kill her with my own hands. Nothing will stand in our way."

"I trust your judgment, Anthony. You will someday be known as the greatest American President." He lifted his glass. "To greatness." He took a long swallow.

"And to you, my friend. You will be right beside me in the Cuban people's greatest moment of triumph." Kirk drained his glass.

7

HOUDINI FAKED HIS DEATH?

Larry King studied the well-dressed man sitting next to him. His interview with Walter Cronkite was going well. The newsman always made an interesting guest. He had talked to presidents, world leaders, and had been America's most trusted reporter for a long time. Yet, he was humble and unassuming when he talked of his exploits. Cronkite seemed to be an expert on all things. They'd already discussed the Vietnam War, problems in the Middle East, and inflation. It was time to deal with something on a lighter note.

King pushed back his eyeglasses. "Let's talk about a completely different subject. Halloween marks the fortieth anniversary of the death of Harry Houdini. It's also National Magic Day, which was started by magicians and is celebrated each year to keep the memory of Houdini alive. There's been a lot of talk about him lately and, of course, psychics have been trying to contact him for years. Gleason's been hinting that something bizarre will happen on his Halloween special, and people are buzzing about it. With all the things going on today, do you find the public's obsession with the magician a little silly?"

Cronkite tapped a finger on the table. "Not at all. Anyone who did as much as Houdini in his lifetime and is still a legend today is newsworthy." Cronkite chuckled. "I would have loved to have interviewed him. He was fascinating, and I'm not sure America really understood Houdini. Thirty minutes or an hour of airtime wouldn't begin to delve into the mind of this man. Just think of his life. He was born in Budapest, Hungary, came to America as an infant, grew up poor as the son of a Rabbi, and became one of the world's greatest entertainers. There were so many facets to him—Houdini the simple, honorable man with a strong devotion to his mother. Houdini the egotist and ruthless self-promoter. Houdini the scholar and crusader against fraud and charlatanism. People that knew him described him as an annoying, likable, and unpredictable genius. He was a complex riddle that makes him a fascinating subject even forty years after his death. His reputation today is stronger than ever."

"It is pretty amazing, isn't it?"

"Well, for many people he symbolizes the American dream. He began with nothing but courage and a belief in his own genius, which amounted to obsession. He was a hero who performed miracles. He became the idol of millions, a friend to presidents, and an entertainer of monarchs."

"What was this thing he had against psychics?"

"During the last few years of his life he'd always use part of his stage act to expose the heartless tricks psychics played on people. It came from his intense love of his mother. When she died, he went to various spiritualists trying to contact her. Several pretended they had, and this infuriated Houdini. His mother didn't speak English, and he knew the exact words she would use to address him. They defrauded him and countless others. I remember one story he told about a father who actually killed his three children because a psychic pretended to channel the dead mother and claimed she wanted her children with her. This was heartbreaking to Houdini."

"It would be heartbreaking to anyone."

"Houdini singled out specific psychics he felt defrauded him and destroyed them. When he went to a new town, he'd wear a disguise and visit local mediums. Then he would expose them by name on stage. He single handedly ruined a lot of lives. Houdini had a dark side. If he became your enemy, he was a formidable one. People who said negative things about him, or tried to fool him, learned that very quickly. The funny thing was, when he was a teenager he thought of using some of the tricks psychics did to make money, but his father wouldn't allow it. Even during his early days in Vaudeville he did a simple mind reading act with his wife, Bess."

"But he didn't believe in psychic powers at all?"

"Oh, he did, but he felt most people in the profession were conmen. He worked hard toward the end of his life to expose them. He got into feuds with some very famous people who disagreed with him. Sir Arthur Conan Doyle was one."

"If you had interviewed him, would you have gotten him to reveal how he did his tricks?"

"Houdini was a master illusionist and unfortunately when he died he had many secrets. A lot of people have speculated on how he performed his magic. I'm not sure there's any living person who would be able to figure out how most of his exploits were really done. If they could, and then performed them, they would become known as the world's greatest magician. I'll leave you with a quote from Houdini: 'The secret of showmanship consists not in what you really do, but what the mystery loving public thinks you do.' The man was a true genius."

RABBI WEISS'S STUDY – MIAMI BEACH

Rabbi Weiss sat in a burgundy armchair jotting into a notebook. Last night, in bed, sleep had eluded him. Lying in the darkness, events crowded his mind, each moment more vivid, more sharply etched than in reality. He'd thought back to his childhood and the hopes, fears, and frustrations that he'd faced. The gun aimed at him almost stopped his heart, but he was an old man and could have accepted death. A bigger part of his unease arose from guilt that he hadn't done enough to conceal his true identity, and his mistakes could have cost others their lives. It was true that after forty years of hiding he'd become complacent. His talks with Gleason about coming out of retirement were based on his ego and desire to once again be in the spotlight before he died. Now he had another reason to do the show.

He had much to get ready before his appearance, but he was tired. The strains of the past few days made him feel older than his years. He wrote another thought into his notebook and then took a sip of water from his crystal goblet. He might only have one chance to speak out, something he should have done long ago, and he intended to use it. If he sat back and said nothing he would surely be killed. It was time to take the offensive. He'd been a fighter all his life.

The police had been back to interview him a second time yesterday. He'd told them as much as he could, holding back the most important piece of his knowledge. They'd learn it tomorrow night on the Gleason show with everyone else.

A knock on the study door interrupted his thoughts. Karen, his housekeeper, pushed open the door.

"You have a visitor," she said.

Weiss got up and recognized Stanford standing behind her. He winced when he noted the young magician's jeans and flowery black and red shirt. Surely he had better clothes to wear than this. "Show the young man in."

Stanford entered the study carrying the two books Weiss had lent him. Shaking Weiss's hand he said, "Your housekeeper is very protective of you."

"She's been with me for many years. With all that's happened recently that's natural." He looked at Karen. "Actually, I don't know what I'd do without her. She knows my schedule better than I do." He put his hand on Stanford's shoulder. "It's so nice to see you again."

Karen smiled and closed the door behind her as she left.

"I'm so sorry to hear about the loss of your temple," Stanford said.

Weiss sat on the edge of his desk, making sure there were no wrinkles in his white shirt. "God sometimes works in mysterious ways. We'll rebuild the temple, and it will be more glorious than ever before, but I appreciate your kind words. Property can always be replaced. It's human life that's really sacred."

"Isn't that the truth." Stanford glanced at the books on the shelves and studied them for a moment. "Theology, history, and magic. You have varied interests, Rabbi."

"I have an inquisitive mind."

Stanford handed Weiss the two books. "I've come to return these. Thanks for allowing me to look at them."

Weiss took the books and placed them on his desk behind him. "I trust you got out of them what you needed."

"Oh, that and much more. They were incredible. Houdini was more amazing than I thought. No one had his stamina, agility, and showmanship. The books taught me what I can be like if I devote myself to the craft."

Weiss's eyes twinkled. "It would take many years of hard work to be even half as good as Houdini."

"I had hoped the books might reveal Houdini's greatest trick, the Water Torture Cell Escape."

Weiss looked annoyed for a moment. "It wasn't a trick. It was an illusion. There's a difference."

"Whatever, Rabbi. I could get some real good gigs if I learned how to do it."

"That illusion cost the man his life. Surely you wouldn't be foolish enough to attempt it."

"What's life without a little risk? Besides, we both know that illusion didn't kill Houdini. As a matter of fact, I don't think he died at all."

Weiss studied Stanford for a few moments. "You have an inquisitive mind, too, but unfortunately logic doesn't seem to be your strong suit. Houdini's death certificate, the reports from his personal physician, and his massive funeral attended by thousands are proof the magician died. Do you think Houdini faked his death?"

Stanford pushed his hand through his shock of brown hair. "For a man who convinced millions that magic existed through his illusions, it wouldn't have been a difficult feat. With enough money you can convince most people to do anything and keep their mouth shut. Particularly if the person offering the cash is a legend."

"If Houdini didn't die where has he been for forty years?"

"Now that's the real question." Stanford pointed toward the two books on the desk. "There are photos inside the books, Rabbi. Your resemblance to Houdini is remarkable."

"Maybe there is a slight resemblance." The answer was quick, too defensive.

"It's more than a slight resemblance. I'd be interested in hearing about your background. I know you've been in Miami for almost forty years, but where were you before? I asked a few people and no one seems to know much about your past. You're a very mysterious man."

"All men are mysterious. It's not our past that's important, but what we do now."

"Were you born in America, Rabbi?"

Weiss didn't answer at first. He stared out the window and his expression hardened. "I was born in Wisconsin. My father was a Rabbi and my mother a remarkable woman who could do anything. They instilled in me the need to help others. I wanted to be a religious man for as long as I can remember."

"Houdini's father was a Rabbi, and the family name was Weiss. Are you sure you weren't born in Budapest, Hungary?"

Weiss smiled. "I think I know where I was born."

"Houdini used to lie about his birth. He claimed to be born in Appleton, Wisconsin. He pretended he was the all American entertainer when actually he was born in Eastern Europe."

"I'm aware of that. Houdini wanted to create an image. Certainly you can understand that."

Stanford pointed to a scar on Weiss's arm. "Could I take a closer look at that?"

Weiss pulled his arm closer to his side. "What interest could you have in a scar I got in an accident years ago?"

"There's always been a rumor that Houdini had an emergency key imbedded into his forearm under his skin that was barely visible. It was said that Houdini went to great trouble to make sure no one could see the key during his act and had only used it when his brute strength and agility failed him. He dug the key out of his arm with his fingers."

For a moment, the only sounds in the room were the wind whipping through the trees and the rattling window. Then Weiss said, "That's a wonderful story, but like most rumors about Houdini, probably not true. As we both know there are many ways to break locks and most of them don't require a key."

"But, some do. Houdini was never one to take chances. He believed that one failure would ruin his career." Stanford studied the Rabbi. "There have also been rumors swirling lately that Houdini is not only alive but planning a return to show business."

"Wouldn't that be ridiculous for him to do? Even if he were alive he'd be an old man now."

Stanford nodded his chin toward Weiss. "He'd be about your age, and you must admit, you're in great shape. Maybe a man your age couldn't perform all the illusions, but even a glimpse of the old Houdini magic would drive the crowd wild. Someone with Houdini's reported ego would love to bask in the adulation of his greatest trick. Hiding out for forty years."

"What you're saying is absurd."

"I don't think so. We magicians know that once show business gets into your blood you have a need to perform that you never lose." He hesitated. "I didn't come here to spar with you, Rabbi. I know you're Harry Houdini. The resemblance, giving me the books on Houdini, your interest in magic, and the scar on your forearm have convinced me. You mentioned at the theater that you might have something to tell me today. I'm ready to listen."

Weiss's gaze wandered, once again, to the window. Tomorrow night, on the Gleason show, he'd tell the world the truth, but he was still reluctant to reveal his true identity to Stanford. After all, what did he really know about him? Could he be trusted? Would he use his knowledge to reveal Houdini's identity before the television show for his own publicity? That could be dangerous.

Weiss's face whitened and he lowered his head.

"Rabbi? Are you all right?"

Weiss waved his hand. "I'm okay."

"Are you sure? You look ill."

"I'm a little dizzy. That's all."

"You should lie down."

"I don't need to lie down. Just give me a minute to clear my head."

"Did you eat breakfast this morning?"

"Uh . . . Sort of. I haven't had much of an appetite lately. Maybe I drank too much coffee."

"Are you sure that's all it is. It could be the stress of the past few days."

Weiss forced a smile. "It'll pass. See what you have to look forward to when you're older?"

Weiss took several deep breaths and the color returned to his cheeks. Then he took a long gulp of water. He'd always believed he'd live to be one hundred, but lately his health had been failing.

"You were about to admit to me that you were Houdini."

Weiss chuckled. "You do have determination. Even if I were Houdini why would I reveal it to you?"

"Because I impress you with my magic, and I believe the rumors that you're going to perform again. It's just a matter of time before you reveal your true identity to the world. Why not tell me a few days early?"

Weiss shook his head. "I am a Rabbi. That you think I'm

Houdini is flattering, but the temple is my theater and, once we rebuild, it will be the only place I will ever perform. You're a creative young man with a vivid imagination. I admire that in you, but don't let a few coincidences carry you to the wrong conclusion."

"You can deny it all you want, but I know the truth. I would like the benefit of your wisdom, sir. It could be an advantage to both of us. You and I together would be the greatest duo magic has ever seen. It would be your chance to get back into the limelight. I would be your protégée."

Weiss rested his hand on his knee. "Now you're really not making sense."

Stanford stood straighter. "My intention is to become the new Houdini and hopefully, someday, people will have the same respect for me they once felt for you. Don't you miss it?"

"I enjoy my life as it is, but how would you become the new Houdini? Surely you don't think you could ever equal him?"

"Possibly in time, but first I will do it by performing the Water Torture Cell Escape on Halloween evening exactly forty years after Houdini's reported death. I will be lowered into the Atlantic, and I will survive. All the news sources will publicize my escape. Everyone will compare me to Houdini."

"It takes many years to be compared to a legend. Houdini struggled during his early years and only by trial and error did he learn to work an audience and develop his reputation."

"Well, I can't wait many years. I want it all now, and I have the ability to achieve it. Performing the Water Torture Cell Escape will create publicity and then people will recognize my talent."

"You do have Houdini's confidence, but the illusion is too dangerous. Only a fool would try to perform it without practicing it for years. Houdini trained for the illusion by practicing similar feats on a smaller scale. Gradually he built up his stamina so he was able to perform the Water Torture Cell Escape."

"I'm young and strong. I could do this illusion. I intend to follow in your footsteps, but I'll only survive if you explain to me how it's done."

The room was cool, yet Weiss felt a trickle of sweat on his forehead. "I've studied that illusion. There are too many things that could go wrong. It's not something you could learn in a day."

"Well, man. I intend to perform that feat of magic whether you help me or not. I have found a box just like the one you used forty years ago. I'll be on the beach tomorrow night, and I'll have my hands cuffed and my legs chained as the box is pushed off the pier into the Atlantic. I realize I don't have much time to perfect the illusion, but I'm a fast learner. How about making things easier for me?"

Weiss stood up. "Listen to me. That illusion killed many men, and failure means a tragic death."

"I don't know the meaning of the word failure."

Weiss took a long, deep breath. "Houdini once felt that way."

"Then we have a lot in common."

Weiss didn't respond.

"You are Houdini, aren't you? Even if you refuse to help me, at least give me that much."

Weiss stared off into space. Maybe it was time. He'd toyed with the idea of revealing his identity to Stanford over the past few days. Maybe they could help one another. "If the attempts on my life this week have proved anything it's that my identity is no longer secret. Yes, you're right. I am Houdini."

Stanford broke into a wide grin. "I knew it. Solea said I was having acid flashbacks when I told her what I thought. Your secret is safe with me until you decide to reveal it to the rest of the world."

"Now that I've told you the truth, I need a special favor. Well, actually two. Will you grant them to me?"

"If I can, sure."

"You are a magician and understand the bond we masters of illusion have. If you respect my magic, you will not try the Water Cell Torture Illusion. That's my first favor."

"No can do. I do respect your magic, and that's why I must perform this feat. Surely you know the importance of magicians being unique and setting themselves apart from all others. I will do it in your honor, but to get it right I need your help."

"Impossible. It would be too painful for me to watch that illusion performed again. I've never revealed what really happened that day to anyone. I swore I'd take it to my grave, but my death may be closer than I thought. Your determination to perform this is foolhardy. Maybe you're just crazy enough to survive, but there are grave risks."

"This is why I need your help."

Weiss shook his head. For a moment, his dizziness returned, and he felt too weak to argue. "I want you to listen carefully to my second favor." He hesitated, wondering how to phrase what he needed. "If I share with you the truth about what happened that day forty years ago, will you promise to tell people the full details if I die before I'm able to do it?"

"First of all, a man in as good a shape as you are will live a long time. If you're thinking those goons that attacked you the other night might try again, they'd have to be totally nuts to attempt it, but I give you my word I'll tell people if you are unable."

Weiss stared out the window for several long seconds. His mind drifted back forty years to the horrible moment when he'd learned the truth. "Things had gotten so crazy for me and Bess that she insisted I fake my death to save my life. I would have done anything for her. I planned an elaborate hoax. What most people don't know is that I performed the trick differently that night. After I was locked into the lid, and before I was lowered into the water, we closed the curtain briefly to make a substitution. Then we reopened it and my brother, Dash, was submerged into the tank. Forty years ago the cell was his tomb."

"Your brother?"

"Yes. He performed the illusion in my place because of the poison."

"Whoa. You're getting ahead of me. What poison?"

"Earlier that day someone tried to poison me. Psychics and mediums considered me an enemy because I exposed them. There were rumors they wanted me dead, and one of them tried to kill me. The stomach pain was excruciating. Still, I was going to go on with my show, but my brother talked me out of it and went in my place. He was supposed to escape just as I would have. He had been my assistant many times and was familiar with my magic. We look so much alike the audience assumed it was me in the tank. Then something went wrong. I think my enemies sabotaged my locks as well. I thought my brother was safe when I pretended to die in Bess's arms. It was the second saddest day of my life, the first being when my mother died."

"But your assistants knew of the substitution. They never told anyone?"

"They were loyal to me and knew if they spoke about what really happened that night it would cost me my life."

"And the psychics attempted to kill you because you tried to expose them?"

"Partially, but I've always felt it was bigger than that. Psychics I could have fought against. It seemed more like a conspiracy."

"You mean a government conspiracy?"

"Not our government, but possibly a foreign one."

"Why would a foreign government want to get rid of you?"

Weiss shrugged. "It's probably just the vivid imagination of an old man."

"But how did you manage to convince people you had died?"

"The same as I did in all my illusions. People see what they expect to see. They thought Houdini died that day, and it didn't take much to convince them. Some suspected, but my brother, by Jewish tradition, was buried quickly. No one could prove what some thought. And of course there was no autopsy. It became imperative for me to disappear so I came here to Miami, hid out, changed my appearance somewhat, and as a way to honor my father who was a Rabbi, and my dead brother, I've devoted myself to good deeds. I've led an honorable life, and no one suspected who I was until recently."

"Man, just like the Vietnam War protesters who went to Canada, you just disappeared. Only a man with your willpower and ability could have pulled it off. I can't tell you how impressed I am."

Weiss waved the compliment off. "But, now things have changed and I am being forced to step forward. You were right about my coming out of retirement."

"Oh, man. This is even better than I could have imagined. You mean I'll actually get to see you perform some magic?"

"Tomorrow night I will appear on the Jackie Gleason show to reveal the truth about the people who have been trying to kill me and cost the life of my brother. One person in particular is behind the latest attempt on my life. I have no proof yet, but by the time of the show, I hope to and will reveal the name to everyone. The citizens of Florida will be very surprised when I unmask him."

"The Gleason show. Man, I've dreamed of being on the Gleason show, but aren't you taking a big chance using that time to name a killer?"

Weiss slowly nodded. "My hope is that once the name is revealed it will be too dangerous for the person to come after me." He hesitated. "So, you see, it will do no good for you to perform the Water Torture Cell Escape tomorrow night. No one will read about it, and all the headlines will be Houdini lives."

"But this is even better. Think of the comparisons that will be made when I successfully perform your greatest illusion on the night you reappear. I must learn the trick. Please help me."

Weiss banged his fist on the table in a rare show of anger. "No. You won't survive. Haven't you heard a word I said? You need many hours of training to be successful. It's one of the most complex illusions ever performed. It was my obsession to always do a better trick that led to my downfall. Don't make the same mistake."

Stanford smiled, his mind made up. "If you won't help me I'll figure out how to do it on my own. Nothing is going to keep me from my destiny of being the new Houdini."

8

My Love Is an Obstacle

Larry King stared at each of the Beatles. They were longhaired, fresh faced, and bizarrely dressed. *What's with the velvet around the sport jacket collars?* he thought. He'd heard a few of their songs and hadn't been impressed, but they were big news and it had been a coup to get them on his show.

He'd already asked about their music and what they thought of America. Everything seemed to be a joke with them, and he wasn't used to interviewing young men who'd become famous so fast. John Lennon was the most talkative of the four, with Paul McCartney a close second. Ringo Starr spoke occasionally, but he'd had to work hard to get anything out of George Harrison. He was running out of questions and still had fifteen minutes to kill. The producer pointed a finger at him.

King waved his hand toward the group to quiet them. "We're back. Our special guests tonight are the Beatles. They'll be appearing at the Mau Mau Room in the gorgeous hotel Deauville in Miami Beach. What do you guys think of Miami?"

John pushed back his round glasses. "We like any city that invites us to perform and pays us, mate, but it is a little quiet for our tastes. People keep talking about this Harry Houdini. Don't they have anything better to do than rattle on about a bloody dead guy?"

"He's big news here. There's speculation that something amazing is going to happen concerning Houdini on the Jackie Gleason Show on Halloween night. Part of it may be just Gleason trying to get publicity, but whatever it is, it's working. Is it just here in Miami that he's big news or have you heard him mentioned elsewhere on your tour of the states?"

"The only thing we've seen on this trip is screaming girls," Lennon said. "I think I'm going a little deaf, so if people are talking about Houdini I wouldn't be able to hear them. Who's Harry Houdini, anyway?"

King's eyebrows shot up a notch. "You do know who Houdini is, don't you?"

Lennon looked at Paul McCartney. "I thought you said Larry had no sense of humor." He refocused on King. "Of course we know Houdini. American culture did make it across the ocean. But he died long ago, and that people are still talking about him is amazing. If there were four of him he could have had his own singing group and outsold us."

"Called himself The Tricksters," Ringo said.

Paul McCartney leaned into the microphone and sang, "I want to break your lock. Yeah. Yeah. Yeah."

John tapped his finger on the table. "He was a big star sure, but seventy-five million people watched us on the Sullivan show. Could Houdini top that?"

"I doubt it," King said. "George, what's your take on Houdini?"

"He certainly knew how to get his name in the paper. Maybe we should use his publicist."

King smiled. "Publicity is not something you guys need more of."

"Houdini had a dark side, ya know?" John said. "There wasn't anything he wouldn't do for free publicity." He laughed. "In that sense he's a lot like the four of us. If I knew how to hang over a bloody street in a strait jacket, I'd do it."

Paul laughed. "And the three of us would help you break out of it. If you weren't free in a month, we'd get you down. Maybe."

"My mates. Always looking out for me. Seriously, no one was bigger than Houdini. He was as popular in his time as we are now, and we're more popular than Jesus. Whoops. I already got into trouble for saying that, didn't I? I'm only kidding folks. Thing is, if Houdini did come back from the dead we'd have some serious competition."

"Well, I don't think there's much chance of that. What are you guys doing next?"

George leaned close to the microphone. The quiet Beatle hadn't said much, and the others looked at him in surprise. "We're going back to England to start our first feature film. I think we're going to call it 'A Hard Day's Night'."

"There you go, George," John said. "That wasn't so hard, was it? Notice how we let him speak, Larry, if he's going to plug something we're working on. Houdini would be proud of you, George."

"Did you know Houdini was a film star?"

"No kiddin'?" John said.

"Sure. Good magic depended on acting ability. Very often it was how difficult a magician made a trick look that swayed the audience. Houdini did a serial called 'The Master Mystery'. He played Quentin Locke, who kept escaping from everything he was put in."

"Clever name," John said.

"But his first full length film, called *The Grim Game*, was made in 1920. That's a little before your time."

"Cheery title," John said. "Did it make any money? That's always the important question."

"No, but he followed it up with a few others. *Terror Island, The Man From Beyond*, and *Haldane of the Secret Service*. It didn't take him long to realize he wasn't cut out for the movies and to go back to the stage."

"Paul's not a film star either," Ringo said, "but that's not stopping him from appearing in a flick."

There was a moment of silence. King wasn't sure what to ask next. Finally he said, "So, what have you guys been doing besides rehearsing for your shows?"

"We never rehearse," John said. "It messes up our playin'. Besides, no one can hear us over the screaming girls. Actually, we did go out to Cassius Clay's training camp the other day. He told us we may be the greatest, but he was the prettiest. Now, there's a man who could give Houdini a run for his money on how to create publicity."

DIPLOMAT HOTEL – MIAMI BEACH

Stanford paced the hotel room, his hair messed, his clothes disheveled. Solea sat on the edge of the bed.

"Will you calm down," Solea said. "Why are you so agitated? At least he admitted he was Houdini."

"I knew that already, but he refused to help me with the Water Torture Cell Escape. It's imperative that I learn it before tomorrow so that it'll be part of all the publicity he gets by being on the Gleason show. I can't understand why he won't help. Can't he see it would be beneficial for both of us? When he was younger, there was nothing he wouldn't do to get his name mentioned. So why won't he help me do the same? The timing of my doing the trick is perfect."

"Of course he refused. He knows you couldn't learn that trick so quickly. He realizes only a fool would attempt to do it with so little training, and he didn't want any part of that. Not helping shows he cares what happens to you. You always said Houdini was a great man. You must listen to him."

"Maybe he was great once, but now he's just an old man who wants to play it safe. He's probably a little jealous of my skills knowing I can do things he'll never be able to do again. Well, it doesn't matter anyway. Even without his help I'll perform the trick. I've got a pretty good idea of how it's done."

Solea's face reddened. "Do you hear what you're saying? You've become obsessed with this. You're not thinking clearly. You will die if you attempt this."

"Die? Oh, give me a break. Houdini performed it many times. How difficult could it be?"

"You'll be under water in heavy chains while trying to break free from handcuffs. How long do you think you'll be able to hold your breath?"

"Houdini could do it for three minutes. I can do it for at least that. I'll be free of the locks by then."

"How many men have been killed trying to recreate Houdini's trick. A dozen? Two dozen?"

"They didn't have my talent. Nothing will happen to me."

"Yes, it will. I've had visions. I see you surrounded by water, drowning with no way to escape."

Stanford raised his voice. "You and your visions. You keep talking about them, but the only time I hear anything specific is when there's something you don't want me to do. Then it's always your vision crap."

Solea's anger flared. "It's not crap. I don't understand the visions myself. Ever since my father died, I've had them. Not very often, but enough to prove to me they mean something. I'm afraid for you, Stanford. I'm trying to save your life."

"I took a chance on you, Solea. When I gave you this job as my assistant you had no experience, but I trained you. I had good judgment then, and I still do. I didn't intend to fall in love with you. It just happened, but I can't let you control my every move. I'm a free spirit, just like Houdini."

A tear ran down Solea's cheek. Stanford moved beside her on the bed and kissed it away. He hated to see her upset. Putting his arms around her he said, "I'm sorry. I didn't mean to come on so strong, but this is important to me."

Solea pulled away. "And I'm not?"

Stanford touched her face and then flicked back her hair. "Of course you are. How can you even say that?"

"Then prove it by promising you won't do the trick."

"I can't."

Solea sat straighter. "Then I will be forced to leave you. I love you, but I refuse to sit back and watch you destroy yourself. You're changing, Stanford. Can't you see that? This obsession with Houdini and his trick has made you lose sight of reality."

"You don't understand what it was like growing up poor and alone. You always had your big Spanish family to support you. My parents ignored me, and I spent most of my time in my room practicing magic and daydreaming. I vowed someday I'd make something of myself. Well, my dream is about to come true. There's no stopping it. I must take advantage of this amazing opportunity I have."

"Aren't I part of your dream now?"

Stanford sighed. "Certainly, and I want you with me when it all comes true. What I need is support, but you keep throwing obstacles at me."

"My love is an obstacle?" She looked away for an instant. "When we first met I had decided not to like you. You were arrogant, I told myself. But there was something about your childish innocence that got through to me. I've always been attracted to strong men. Men who knew what they wanted in life and went after it. You're that way, Stanford. It's what makes me want to be with you, but there's such a thing as going too far. You're being foolhardy."

"Foolhardy? I can do this. I've mastered the individual parts. It's just a question of putting everything together. Sure, I wish I had more time to practice and the benefit of Houdini's guidance, but it's only an illusion. This kind of opportunity comes along only once in a lifetime. If I let it pass I'll always look back and wonder what would have happened if I'd taken the chance."

"Things are not that simple anymore. Can't you see that? Being a couple means compromise and giving up something because the other is strongly against it. You seem willing to give me up because you'll get a lot of publicity by doing Houdini's trick. You have talent, charisma, and ambition. You don't need some gimmick to get noticed. Sure, right now it would be good for your career. That's if by some miracle you managed to survive. But, I won't be around to share your good fortune. Is that what you want?"

Stanford glanced toward the hotel window and took a long, deep breath. "I don't want to lose you. Don't make me choose. We can have it all if you stay with me."

Solea shook her head. "You must choose. If you decide to perform this dangerous trick, I'll leave you. There is your choice. Should I pack?"

Stanford stared at her for a long moment, his mind churning. "You leave me little choice. All right, I won't do the trick. Does that make you happy?"

Solea arched her eyebrows. "You gave in quickly."

"I know what's important to me. When you said it the way you did I realized there was no choice."

Solea kissed him passionately. "I love you, Stanford."

Stanford ran his finger across her lips. "Now, go take a shower. I'm taking you out on the town."

Solea walked into the bathroom and a few minutes later the shower was turned on.

Stanford stretched out on the bed, staring at the ceiling. Then he rolled over, picked up the phone, and dialed. "It's a definite. I will be performing the Water Torture Cell Escape tomorrow night. I've got to spend some serious rehearsal time until then." He listened for a few seconds. "Yes, I'm aware how dangerous it is. Now you sound like Solea. I need you to call every newspaper and television person you know. I want thousands of people at the Hallover Pier to watch me perform the world's most dangerous trick. Oh, and if you see Solea, don't mention it to her. I want to keep it a secret from her for as long as I can."

He hung up the phone and pushed his body back on the pillows. Solea's insistence that he not perform the trick bothered him. Sure, it was dangerous, but there seemed to be something else at work here. Again his suspicion that she had a secret entered his mind. Could it be possible? As Solea sang in the shower, his thoughts drifted back to how they'd met on the beach. Did even that random event have a more sinister purpose?

The first night they had dinner he'd been struck with her beauty and charm. After a few drinks, he told her about his life and secret dreams. He opened up to her in a way he'd never done with any woman. There was something about her innocence and enthusiasm that made him want to tell her everything. He told her about his loneliness, and how his mother threw his father out after years of abuse when he was seventeen. Part of Stanford's drive and ambition was pushed by his desire to prove to his mother that he could make something of himself.

He'd asked about her life in Barcelona and what her uncle in Miami was like. She'd evaded his questions, and although Stanford wondered why, he didn't press her on it.

It didn't take much convincing to get her to work with him. It was almost as if she'd made up her mind beforehand. As he trained her, he found that not only was she beautiful and agile but a quick learner as well. And he realized he was falling in love with her, something he hadn't counted on.

Still, there were things about her that troubled him. During the week they'd known each other she'd still not shared much of her private life. He found her reticence unnatural considering how close they'd become.

The running water in the shower turned off, snapping him back to the present. Maybe it was just his imagination, but he didn't think so. He made up his mind to find out more about her. The thing was, if she wouldn't tell him he wasn't quite sure how to go about it.

He got up, went to the window, and looked out over the beach. Solea's purse rested on a chair. The clasp was open and a slip of paper was visible. He reached in and pulled it out. A local phone number was written next to the name Uncle Anthony. He glanced back toward the ocean. He was sure she'd told him her uncle's name was Fernando.

9

IS GREAT YOUR FIRST NAME?

"Welcome to the Larry King Show. My guest tonight is Sammy Davis Jr. He's a singer, dancer, and a comedian. A real triple threat. Thanks for dropping by, Sammy. What brings you to town?"

"I'm with my pal, Sinatra, and we're doing a gig over at the Fontainebleau. He allows me to sing a few songs during the middle of his set as long as I don't upstage him. He comes out first and likes me to sit in the audience, cheer loudly, and yell, 'You're the greatest entertainer of all time, Frank.' You know how insecure Sinatra can be. It's always a trip to be in Miami, but this seems like a particularly groovy time to be here."

"It is. I'm sure you've heard the rumors swirling about Harry Houdini. It seems to be all anyone can talk about. With tomorrow being Halloween, the anticipation of what might happen on the Gleason show is rising. Do you think it's some kind of publicity stunt, or do you think there's some substance when people say the magician's alive?"

"Hey, man, I'm just a one-eyed black Jew. Who's going to listen to me?"

"There is a connection between your family and Houdini."

"You mean you want me to reveal the family secret that Houdini was my brother?"

King laughed. "No, the other connection."

"Oh, that one. Well, my dad started out in Vaudeville, and he and Houdini played some of the same theaters—the 14th Street

Theater and The Eschler Music Hall in New York City, and The Hopkins Theater in Chicago."

"Vaudeville was tough, wasn't it?"

"How old do you think I am, man? I'm far too young to remember, but my dad used to tell stories. There'd be fifteen or twenty acts on a bill and sometimes they'd do the same routine twenty times a day. It was difficult to get noticed and stand out from the other acts. The pay was awful, and the competition was cut throat. A lot of people gave up. My dad said Houdini's exploits in Vaudeville were legendary. He was convinced he was the greatest act on the bill, and when an audience didn't treat him that way he grew more determined. That's when he started doing all those publicity stunts to get noticed. The man had persistence and would do any type of gig he was asked to, including a mind reading act. There were times things were so tough he had to steal potatoes so he and Bess could eat. But he had balls. Sorry. Can I say balls on the radio?"

King shook his head slowly. "You just did. Twice."

Davis smiled and pushed back his horn-rimmed glasses. "The thing about Houdini was he really felt it was just a matter of time before the public realized how good he was and he became famous. Man, was he right."

"Some people are expecting Houdini to put in an appearance on the Gleason show. It seems a little far fetched, doesn't it?"

"If he does, I hope he'll consider opening for me when I play New York City next week. Two Jewish guys on the same bill. We'll pack 'em in."

STANFORD'S HOTEL ROOM – MIAMI BEACH

Solea walked out of the bathroom wearing a low cut, red evening gown. Her long hair was curled and hung to her shoulders. She spread her arms and did a slow twirl.

Stanford looked up from the book he was reading and his eyes widened. "My God. You look amazing."

Solea reached out her hand. "Take me out on the town. We have a lot to celebrate."

As they locked the hotel room door, Stanford thought about

the phone number in Solea's purse. He was curious, but he wasn't about to let anything spoil their night.

They exited the hotel and crossed the parking lot. The night was warm and clammy, the smell of salt in the air. Stanford eyed his 1963 powder blue Mustang convertible. The vehicle was Stanford's pride. It was the first thing he'd bought when he started making money, and he used it driving from show to show. He put the key in the ignition and the engine roared to life.

"Should I put the top down?" Stanford asked.

"Yes, I want to feel the breeze on my face. This is going to be a magnificent night. I just know it. "

Stanford powered the top down, then punched the accelerator and pulled out into the traffic on Collins Avenue. They cruised past several restaurant and high-rise hotels.

Stanford pointed to a beach. "That's where it all started for us. I thought you were shy at first. Now, when I look back on it, I feel that day it was you who wanted to be with me, and I fell into your trap."

"I seem to remember it differently. You chased after me on the beach."

"But that was after you made sure I saw you."

Solea smiled. "Whatever happened, it changed our lives. I can't tell you how important it is that you decided not to perform Houdini's trick. I would have left you, you know?"

Stanford gripped the steering wheel and kept his eyes focused straight ahead. "Tell me about your uncle. You've only mentioned him once. His name's Fernando, right?"

Solea glanced nervously at him. "Oh, Uncle Fernando's a poor, humble man. There's nothing much to tell. He, too, lived in Barcelona for a few years. He's been helpful to me, but he can't take care of me forever. That's why I agreed to work with you so willingly."

"Is he the only relative you have in the area?"

"Yes. Why the sudden interest?"

"I'm interested in everything about you."

"Oh, Stanford. Let's not talk about anything serious tonight. I just want to have fun."

Stanford glanced into the rearview mirror, noting a dark sedan behind them. Was it his imagination or had this same car been following since they left the hotel? His normally suspicious mind seemed to be at full throttle.

Stanford got a bad feeling. Was Solea hiding something from him? Did she have an Uncle Fernando, and who was this mysterious Uncle Anthony? Maybe she was embarrassed to mention him. But why? When he had the opportunity, he'd track the man down. He had plenty of time to find out what Solea was trying to hide. He was sure it was nothing serious.

Solea flipped on the radio and hummed along to The Temptations' "Ain't Too Proud To Beg." When the song changed to Nancy Sinatra's "These Boots are Made for Walking," Solea tapped the dashboard and sang, "These boots are made for walking, and someday they're going to walk all over you." She looked so happy and innocent.

Stanford pressed harder on the gas and tried to put the doubts out of his mind. Approaching the Fontainebleau Hotel, he pointed to the marquee. "Tonight Frank Sinatra" it read.

"Wow," Stanford said. "It's like karma. Nancy on the radio and Frank at the hotel. He's not as good looking as his daughter, but he is one of the ultimate showmen. Let's go see him. I want to watch how he works the crowd."

Solea's face broke into a wide grin. "I love Frank Sinatra."

Stanford looked at her, a hint of jealousy on his face. They pulled onto the circular driveway and under a canopy in front of the modern high-rise hotel. Stanford glanced toward the street looking for the dark sedan, but it was nowhere in sight. He knew the car shouldn't have bothered him, that it was probably just someone innocent like him just driving through the streets of Miami. Still, he breathed a sigh of relief.

A valet parker opened the door for Solea, checking her legs as she slid off the seat. Then he came around and opened Stanford's door.

Stanford slipped him a bill. "I am The Great Stanford and this is my assistant Solea. Which to Mr. Sinatra's performance?"

The valet parker pointed. "That way."

Solea took Stanford's hand as they entered the hotel. The marble floor of the lobby looked spit shined and the people milling around were well dressed, the women in fancy evening gowns and the men in dark suits. Leather easy chairs and potted plants were scattered about. The room smelled lemony, and the clerks behind the front desk were young and well groomed. Solea stared wide-eyed, as if she'd never seen anything quite like it.

A slender man in his mid-twenties dressed in jeans and a black silk shirt was seated in one of the leather chairs. He had a shock of brown hair longer than Stanford's. His eyes widened as he looked at them and got up as they walked by.

"Excuse me. You're the Great Stanford. I saw you perform at Rabbi Weiss's fundraiser the other night. You were tremendous." He extended his hand. "My name's Steve Wynn."

Stanford was flattered and shook his hand. "Thanks, man."

Wynn fluttered his hand to take in the entire lobby. "What do you think of this place? Isn't it amazing?"

"It is quite beautiful," Solea said. "Are you staying here?"

"Nah, I couldn't afford a place like this. Yet. I'm over at a motel on the other side of town." Wynn smiled at Stanford as if they were great friends. "But, I am going to build a place as big as this someday. It'll be a gambling casino with a spacious theater. People will line up and the dough will roll in."

Stanford didn't like the way Solea looked at the other man. "It's nice to meet another ambitious soul. I wish you luck. Have a good evening."

Wynn walked with them, and Stanford was afraid he planned to follow them into the theater. "Five years from now the name Steve Wynn will be synonymous with lavish luxury. It's great to be ambitious, but you must have vision as well. I'd like to make you a business proposition."

Stanford looked amused. "For what? You haven't built anything yet, have you? Do you want me to play at the motel you're staying at? Besides, I'm booked into early next year."

"Oh, I don't want you now, but when my palace is built. I'd like to sign you to a long-term contract. You have such talent. In a few years, you'll be very famous and my casino will be just as well known. We could grow together. I've even thought of a name for my palace. I'll call it The Mirage. That's the perfect name for a place to have an incredible magic act like yours."

"In a few years you couldn't afford me."

"I wouldn't be so sure about that. Very soon I'll be able to buy and sell a place like the Fontainebleau."

"And where will this wonderful casino be?"

"I'm still working on that. Maybe in New York or LA. Possibly Europe or China. I might even decide on a desert location and build it in a place like Las Vegas in Nevada."

"Why would anyone travel to a small desert town in the middle of nowhere to gamble? Let me make a suggestion to you. Maybe you should rethink your plans and go for something smaller. And you don't need a magician. You'd be better off with a tiger act."

Stanford and Solea walked away. Wynn was right behind them.

"Are you planning on seeing Sinatra?" Wynn asked.

"Yes."

"I hope you have tickets because he's been sold out for weeks. He's the hottest show in town. Sinatra will someday play at my Mirage, as well."

"There is no place The Great Stanford can't get in or out of."

As Wynn walked away he said, "In a couple of years you and I will talk. By then my palace will be well under way."

"Guy's a loser," Stanford whispered. "Staying at a motel and hanging out at the Fontainebleau. Now that's pathetic. I guess I should get used to men like that wanting to sign me."

They approached the tuxedoed host at the entrance to the club.

"We'd like to see Mr. Sinatra," Stanford said.

The host eyed Solea. Then he hardened his expression as he looked back at Stanford. "I'm sorry, sir. Tonight's performance is sold out. You should have gotten tickets in advance."

Stanford reached into his pocket, pulled out a bill, and handed it to him. "I'm The Great Stanford and this is Solea, my assistant. I'm sure Mr. Sinatra has heard of me and would be honored to have me in his audience."

The host shook his head. "Sorry, sir. As I said the room's filled."

Stanford took out another bill.

The host shoveled the money into his jacket. "Sir, I think we just might have a seat up close to the stage. Follow me."

They followed the man and walked by several circular tables covered with white tablecloths. A few luxury leather booths were on the side of the stage. The room was packed, filled with laughter and loud voices, and smelled of cigarette smoke and alcohol.

The host held a chair for Solea. They were three rows from the stage.

"Man," Stanford said, sitting down. "Look at this full house. Someday I'm going to have audiences like this."

He noted a Cuban looking man with jet-black hair and a squat, powerful body entering the room. His eyes locked on Stanford, then he quickly looked away. A feeling of uneasiness passed through Stanford again. Why was he so suspicious of everyone?

After ordering champagne, Stanford noticed Sammy Davis Jr. seated in the rear of the room, talking to another man. Davis puffed on a cigarette and was having an animated conversation.

Stanford tapped Solea's arm. "Follow me. Here's a chance to get some free publicity."

They got up, made their way to the back, and approached Davis. The entertainer was dressed in a brown suit and his white shirt was open, revealing a thick, gold chain.

"Hey, everyone," Stanford yelled. "Look who's here. It's Sammy Davis Jr."

Davis smiled and waved to the crowd, but seemed annoyed. He leaned into Stanford. "Who the hell are you?"

People in the room quieted and focused on the two men. "I'm The Great Stanford. I perform illusions," he said loudly.

"Hey, man. No need to yell. I'm not deaf." He hesitated. "Stanford? I've heard of you. Didn't you do a fundraiser for underprivileged children with Rabbi Weiss the other night?"

"I did. He's a great man. Even greater than most imagine."

"The Rabbi's big-hearted, and that's a wonderful cause. It was terrible what happened after the show. I was glad nothing happened to him. Have you talked to him recently? Is he okay?"

"He's a strong man. I was with him today. He's doing as well as can be expected."

"Give him my best. I've helped him out before. Some of my friends went to the show. I heard your performance was marvelous."

"Thanks. How about doing a trick with me?"

Davis jabbed a cigarette at him. The heavy gold chain around his neck glistened in the overhead lights. "Sure, man. What would you like me to do?"

"Close your eyes. I'm going to levitate you into the air."

Davis backed away. "Oh, no. I like to keep my feet on the ground. The only way I fly is by having a few drinks."

The crowd laughed, not sure if this was part of the show.

Stanford reached inside his coat, pulled out a cane and a top hat. He handed them to Sammy.

"For your next appearance."

"Not bad, but can you make my bar bill disappear."

"Sure. Waiter, put Sammy's tab on Mr. Sinatra's bill."

The crowd applauded. On their way back to their seats, Stanford and Solea stopped at a table. Stanford pulled a coin from behind a man's ear. Then he handed him back his wallet.

"You may need this later."

Two glasses of champagne were on their table as they sat down.

Stanford hoisted his glass. "To success in everything we touch."

Solea smiled and took a sip. Then she said, "I'm going to freshen up before the show starts."

Stanford waited until she left the room then got to his feet. He clapped his hands several times until he had everyone's attention. "If you think the tricks I just did for you were astounding, you must see me perform the Water Torture Cell Escape. I will be handcuffed and lowered into the ocean, upside down, in a water-filled and chained box. It's the greatest trick ever performed. It was Houdini's last trick. I'll be doing it tomorrow night at the Hallover Pier, exactly forty years after the great man's last performance."

"We'll be watching the Gleason show," one man muttered. "He's doing something with the real Houdini."

"Ah. And you don't want to miss that, but come see me first. It won't take me long to complete the illusion and prove I am a worthy successor to the Great Houdini. My performance is at seven. You'll be home in plenty of time to see Gleason."

"You seem pretty sure of yourself," a woman said.

"All good magicians must believe they are invincible. It separates the great ones from the mediocre. But there are always elements of danger. Come see for yourself tomorrow. You be the judge of how good I am."

"Do you know what Gleason's up to?"

"I do, but I'm sworn to secrecy."

"You're foolish to try that trick," another man said.

"Possibly. There are those who think I won't survive." He

moved to the table and approached the man. "Do you think I'll survive?" When the man didn't respond, Stanford waved his hands to the crowd. "I invite you all to come. It'll be something you'll never forget."

As Stanford walked back to his table, he noticed a young man scribbling on a napkin, lost in thought. He was in his early twenties with brown, curly hair, dressed in a dark suit.

"You look familiar to me," Stanford said.

The man glanced up, and then continued to write. "I'm in show business, too. My name's Paul Anka."

Stanford nodded. "Ah. The singer." He pointed to the napkin. "Are you writing a song?"

"I am. I was just backstage talking to Mr. Sinatra. He told me he might retire after putting out one more album. He asked when I was going to write a song for him. It's not everyday I get an opportunity like this."

"As entertainers we must take advantage of everything, but Sinatra will never retire. Once show business is in your blood you never leave."

Anka pushed the napkin toward Stanford. "What do you think of these lyrics?"

Stanford read the first line aloud. "'And now the end is near.' No offense, but they don't seem to apply to Mr. Sinatra. You make it sound like he's about to die. Let me give you some advice. If you want Mr. Sinatra to record your music, you've got to write him a happy song."

When Stanford got back to his table, Solea was waiting. Her complexion was pale.

"Are you all right?" Stanford asked.

Solea nodded, but Stanford knew something was bothering her. Had she heard him talk about the Water Torture Cell Escape?

"What happened?"

Solea looked toward the entrance of the theater. "Do you see that man over there?"

Stanford turned. "Where?"

"He was at the doorway a second ago. It was a man with jet black hair."

"Yeah, I noticed him earlier."

"He watched me when I left the room and as I came back he

said, 'I hope you enjoy the show, Solea.' It was spooky. How did he know my name?"

Stanford remembered his own uneasiness when he'd seen the man and then thought about the car he felt was following them, but he didn't want to alarm Solea.

"He was probably standing near the host when I introduced you, or maybe he was at the show the other night." Stanford smiled. "You're going to have to get used to being recognized. It's part of show business."

Solea's shoulders relaxed. "Oh, you're probably right. Who was that you were talking to?"

"Paul Anka."

"The singer? I loved 'Put Your Head on my Shoulder' and 'Diana.'" She glanced at his table. "He's so cute."

"Ah. But does he have talent? Frankie Avalon, Fabian, Bobby Rydell, Neil Sedaka, Paul Anka. Five years from now no one will remember any of them. He claimed to be writing a song for Sinatra. I looked at a snippet of the lyrics, and believe me, Sinatra would hate it."

"How do you know?"

"Listen to this. 'For what is man, what has he got? If not himself, then he has naught.' What does that mean?"

"I think it's touching."

"Touching? What next? Is he going to write a song about having a baby?"

Before Solea could respond, the lights dimmed and an older man dressed in a tuxedo came out on stage. "Ladies and gentlemen, the Fontainebleau is proud to present a legend, and the man with the velvet voice. Old blue eyes himself. Please welcome Frank Sinatra."

There was loud applause and a few people stood to get a better view. A few camera lights flashed as Sinatra walked on stage and bowed.

He was dressed in a dark gray suit that probably cost more than Stanford's weekly wages. His brown hair was pushed back and thinning, his blue eyes piercing. Although he was skinny, the man still packed plenty of charisma. Several women screamed as if they were teenagers.

Solea clapped wildly, her eyes riveted on Sinatra.

"Thank you for coming. It's great to be in Miami again. This song's for all the ladies in the audience tonight."

The houselights dimmed and a single spotlight shone on the singer. The orchestra started to play "I've Got You Under My Skin." Sinatra snapped his fingers and swayed before starting to sing. The crowd sat at rapt attention. When the song was over, Sinatra bowed and the houselights came up.

"I play all over the world and no audience is better than a Miami Beach one." Sinatra smiled and looked toward the rear of the theater where Sammy Davis, Jr. sat. "That's where I am, right Sammy?"

"That's right, Boss. And you're Frank Sinatra, remember?"

Sinatra laughed. "That's why I keep Sammy around. I saw a magician going from table to table. He even got my good friend Sammy to smile, but that doesn't mean anything. Sammy even laughs at my jokes. Was the magician any good?"

The crowd applauded.

"Where is he?" Sinatra asked. "Put up the house lights so I can see him."

The room brightened as Stanford stood, smiled, and waved. "I think everyone here knows me, Mr. Sinatra, except you. I am The Great Stanford."

"A true entertainer. Notice how he got up? Is Great your first name?"

"No, Stanford is my first name."

"Enough about you. Who's the beautiful woman you're with?"

"Solea, my assistant. She's an important part of my show. She—"

"I'm sure she is." Sinatra held out his hand. "Come up here, beautiful. I want to get a closer look."

Stanford's face reddened, clearly angry. Solea shyly got up and walked the few steps onto the stage.

Sinatra looked her up and down as she approached. "Solea is a lovely name. Spanish, right?"

Solea nodded.

"You are a true Spanish beauty." He pointed to Stanford. "What are you doing with a guy like him? And a magician at that. What you need in your life is a singer like me, and it just so happens I'm between wives. We could make beautiful music together."

Solea glanced at Stanford. "Stanford is a great magician. I enjoy working with him."

"Amazing. A woman as gorgeous as you who enjoys doing magic. How about creating a little magic with me?"

"My real talent is singing."

"And I bet you're very talented."

The crowd laughed. Stanford fidgeted in his chair, not liking the way Sinatra leered at Solea.

"Do you know my song, 'The Way You Look Tonight?'"

"Yes."

"Well, I want to dedicate it to you. Will you to sing it with me?"

"Oh, no. I couldn't."

Sinatra turned to the audience. "Come on. What do you think? Should Solea and I perform together?"

The audience cheered loudly. The orchestra started to play, and Sinatra began the song. He motioned to Solea and she joined in, tentatively at first, but as the music progressed, with more confidence.

Sinatra put his arm around her and pulled her close. When he touched her hair, Stanford had had enough. His anger erupted and he bolted for the stage. Two bodyguards blocked his way, but he eluded them and bounded up the steps. Taking Solea's hand, he pulled her from Sinatra.

The orchestra stopped playing and the house lights came up.

"Hey, Buddy," Sinatra said. "Cool down. It's just part of my act. You're in show business. You know what it's like."

Stanford jabbed a finger at Sinatra. "Well, you stepped over the line."

Solea's face reddened with embarrassment. "Stanford, don't make a scene."

Stanford pulled Solea's arm gently. "Come back to the table."

"I want to sing with Mr. Sinatra. You know how much I love music."

Sinatra smiled. "Frank, honey. Call me Frank."

Stanford dropped Solea's hand and moved closer to Sinatra. "Someday I'll be bigger than you ever were."

"Come back when you grow up, kid."

Stanford clenched his fist, and the bodyguards ran onto the stage. Sinatra moved toward Stanford and waved the bodyguards off. There was no noise in the room. All eyes were focused on the two men.

Stanford stared at Solea for a few seconds. "Solea, I need for you to come with me."

"When the song is over. This is a big opportunity for me. Don't spoil it."

Stanford looked at Sinatra, then glanced at the audience. When he refocused on Solea, he had made a decision. "Solea, will you marry me?"

"Don't talk crazy."

"I'm not. I've been thinking about this since I met you. Seeing you with Sinatra and feeling this intense jealousy for the first time in my life made me realize how much I love you. I always said you don't get what you want unless you go after it. I want you with me always."

Solea looked down at the floor, not responding.

Sinatra moved closer to Stanford. "You want I should make the magician disappear?"

The audience laughed nervously.

"I want to spend the rest of my life making you happy, Solea. No matter what it takes. Think of how glorious it's been up to now. That's nothing compared to what it will be like." He hitched his thumb toward Sinatra. "I'd even fight a man like that to get you."

Solea's mouth opened, but nothing came out.

Stanford knelt on one knee in front of her and took her hand. "What would I have to do to get you to accept? Do I have to beg?"

"This love is dangerous, Stanford," Solea said.

"All love is dangerous, isn't it? I suppose I've been frightened of a commitment to someone special all my life, but I'm beginning to understand now." He looked straight into her face. "You're only half alive if you're afraid to love."

"Solea shook her head. "You simply don't understand what you're asking. This would be more dangerous than you could imagine. What do you really know about me?"

"That doesn't matter. I love you, and whatever obstacles we have to overcome we'll do it together. Do you love me?"

Solea hesitated, then said softly, "Yes."

"Then agree to marry me."

Solea smiled. "Yes, I will marry you."

The crowd erupted in applause and hoots.

Sinatra shrugged and looked at the audience. "You never know what you're going to see at one of my shows, but I'm not sure even I could top this. I wish you kids the best. Maybe I can perform at your wedding. I'll get that Anka kid to write a song especially for you."

Stanford felt giddy. "No. Solea will be the one singing at our wedding."

"I don't know what you have, kid," Sinatra said. "But it must be something to get a beautiful woman like that."

Stanford took Solea's hand and they exited the stage. Walking through the lobby, they left the hotel.

The man with the jet-black hair was pulling out of the parking lot as they got into the Mustang. As Stanford watched the dark sedan drive onto Collins Avenue and disappear into the traffic, he realized who the man on the beach was the day he'd met Solea. He'd seen Anthony Kirk on television and knew the man was being groomed to run for president. It must have been a coincidence that he was walking by the ocean that day.

Surely, he had no connection to Solea.

10

DEATH DEFYING TRICK TO BE PERFORMED

ALLIGATOR PROCESSING PLANT – EVERGLADES, FLORIDA

The man leaned over the table slicing a long, straight incision into the soft underbelly of the alligator with an oversized butcher's knife. His blood-splattered gray apron pulled tight across his stomach as he carved. The cutter was at least fifty pounds overweight, and sweat dripped down his pudgy cheeks. Slowly, he ripped the skin and separated it from the bone.

The room was small, and the long workbench filled most of the space. On the floor was a stack of alligator skins piled to the windowsill. A table, off to the side, was loaded with saws, knives, hammers, screwdrivers, and axes. The coppery smell of blood filled the air.

It was early morning, and the building was located well off the main road on a spit of land surrounded by tall pines. The cutter knew that legitimate processing plants needed to be certified by the state, and he didn't want the regulators to show up on his doorstep. With the drop in the price paid for alligator hides, the cost of being licensed would put him out of business, and he was content to keep his operation small. Luckily, people still paid well for meat, teeth, skulls, and claws from the reptile.

A knock on the door startled him for a moment. With the sun barely breaking the horizon a visitor could only mean one thing. Fresh meat.

He slid the alligator off the table and plopped it onto the floor. Then he stripped off his goggles and rubber gloves.

Opening the door he said, "Emilio. Good morning. I didn't hear you pull up. You're here earlier than usual. Hunting must have been bad. What do you have for me?"

"One," Emilio said entering the room, a look of disgust on his face. "Can you believe it, Billy? A whole night of cruising in my motor boat and that's all I can come up with."

Emilio tugged on his yellow rain slicker. The long hair around the edges of the New York Yankees cap was damp from the morning dew. He was in his early fifties and had been an alligator catcher for years. Like Billy, he did his work illegally.

"I can't remember the last time you brought in only one. Usually you catch at least a half dozen. Did you fall asleep out there?"

"Something spooky was going on last night. Lots of traffic around the swamp. What with car headlights, the rustling of trees, and human voices the gators must have been scared off. I sat with my spear all ready, but little was happening."

"Well, one is better than nothing. I need as many as I can get. Who knows why there were so few? Maybe the gators were having a wild party and didn't invite you. I'm sure you'll do better for me tonight."

Billy opened his wallet, took out a few bills, and slapped them into Emilo's outstretched hand. "I appreciate the business."

Emilio counted the money, then shoveled it into his rain slicker. He shook his head. "Not much for a night's work."

They walked into the humid morning air. Frogs croaked and crickets chirped in the distance. The sun rose over the trees, giving the few clouds a pinkish tinge. The gator was stretched out in the back of the Ford pick up truck and wrapped in clear plastic. Billy took the front while Emilio grabbed the rear. They grunted as they carried it across the gravel driveway. Bringing it inside, they plopped it on the table, belly up.

Billy flipped on a lamp, its yellowish glow reflecting on the reptile. "Usually I like to work in the dim light." He pointed to the lone lamp on a shelf a few feet away, which cast eerie reflections on the wall. "It keeps me focused, but this baby is a big one and I'm going to need more illumination."

He slit the plastic open with his knife and then snapped on his goggles. "Man, he's a good fifteen feet long and must weigh at least four hundred pounds. No wonder we had trouble getting it in from the truck." He pointed with his chin toward the kitchen. "There's coffee where it always is. Help yourself."

Billy slipped on his gloves and bent his head low to examine the alligator. Grabbing a saw from the table, he cut off one of the alligator's limbs. Blood spurted into the air, speckling the wall and dripping to the floor. He studied the limb, then threw it in the corner to work on later. He picked up his serrated butcher's knife again and sliced the gator down the middle, cutting a wide incision and spreading it with his gloved hands.

Emilo entered the room, sipping coffee. "God, how can you stand all the blood?"

"It's a living. Just like you spending your nights alone in the Glades when you could be with a woman. We do what we have to."

Billy scrunched his eyes and moved his head closer to the alligator's stomach. "Looks like the underground is disposing of bodies in alligator alley again."

Emilio put the cup down and approached the table.

Billy reached into the alligator's stomach and pulled out a fully formed bloody hand. The fingers were mangled and bent back; one had been bitten off entirely. Attached to the wrist was a watch smeared with blood. He fumbled to undo the clasp, and then wiped it with a cloth.

"There's an inscription." Billy lifted the watch closer to the overhead lights. "To Renaldo. In appreciation for what you've done for the Cuban people." He shoveled the watch into his apron. "He won't be needing this anymore."

HOTEL DIPLOMAT – HALLOWEEN MORNING

Solea rolled over on the bed and stared at Stanford snoring softly. Had she really agreed to marry him? She moved her hand to within inches of his face and traced an outline of his skull. Her impulsive decision would cause problems with her family. That was one thing she was sure of. Hopefully, Uncle Anthony would understand when she explained it to him.

Quietly she got up and slipped on a pair of jeans and a tee shirt. Then she clasped a small diamond necklace around her neck and admired it. Stanford had bought it for her last night to celebrate their engagement. He promised to buy her a much bigger engagement ring when he could afford it.

She'd only known him for ten days, but the love she felt for him was intense and passionate. He was wild and enthusiastic about life, so unlike other men she'd known. There was an impulsive side to him as well, but she was sure she could tame him in time. After all, he had agreed not to perform Houdini's trick because of her. She took one more look at him and decided she'd surprise him by having coffee for him when he woke up.

Leaving the hotel room, she took the elevator to the lobby in search of coffee. She passed two men standing near the front desk having an animated conversation. One had a flyer in his hand and was waving it at the other.

"I think the man's crazy," he said. "That trick killed Houdini. You've seen the kid. He's a scrawny thing. Don't you think he's a little bizarre?"

Solea stopped in mid-stride and stared at the men. Surely they couldn't be talking about Stanford.

"Bizarre," the other one said, "but not crazy. We all know it's a trick, some kind of illusion. You don't think a magician is actually going to put his life in danger, do you?"

"Houdini did and died because of it. All I know is I'll be on the pier tonight. If something goes wrong I don't want to miss it."

Solea walked to within a few inches of the men. "Excuse me. Who are you talking about?"

The man held up the flyer. "Haven't you heard? That Stanford guy is going to perform Houdini's Water Cell Torture Escape at Hallover Pier tonight at seven."

Solea's heart hammered as she took the flyer and read it. The headline stated, "Death defying trick to be performed tonight." She looked up. "This is a mistake. He changed his mind and decided not to do it."

The man shook his head. "I don't think so. A guy was in the lobby handing those out just a few minutes ago. He said Stanford was definitely going to be there."

Solea's face reddened and her anger flared. Stanford had lied to her. She should have known he'd given in too easily. Last night he'd acted strange, like he was hiding a secret. How could he do this? She had to stop him.

She bounded up the stairs, too impatient to wait for the elevator, and rushed into the room. The shower was running. She put her hand on the doorknob to the bathroom and stopped. What good would it do to confront him? He had lied to her once, he might lie again. Uncle Anthony was right. Magicians couldn't be trusted.

She paced to the window, looked out, and thought of her visions. They'd been so strong and vivid. Stanford would die tonight if he attempted Houdini's trick. She was sure of it. As she listened to him hum in the shower, she knew what she had to do. There was one person she could turn to—the man who'd taken her in when she first came to America, the man who had many friends in the police department. Uncle Anthony would figure out a way to stop him. She grabbed Stanford's car keys and rushed from the room.

Getting the Mustang from the parking lot, she exited the hotel grounds and sped along Collins Avenue. Her eyes filled with tears as she passed the Fontainebleau and saw the marquee advertising Frank Sinatra. She pumped the accelerator and passed several cars, driving recklessly, not caring about her own safety. The tires squealed as she turned onto a side road and pulled into the driveway of a white stucco low-rise house located on the beach. She jumped out of the car, ran to the door, and rang the bell.

11

SOLEA FEARS KIRK

The door snapped open. Anthony Kirk's white knit shirt and white slacks emphasized his tan. His expression hardened for a moment and then he smiled. "Solea." He held his arms open. "What do I owe the honor of this visit? Do you have news for me?" He hesitated and studied her. "What's wrong? You look upset."

Solea pushed by him into the living room. "It's Stanford."

Kirk followed her in. "The young magician? What has he done to you?"

"To me? Nothing. It's what he's planning on doing to himself. He's performing Houdini's Water Torture Cell Escape at Hallover Pier tonight. It's dangerous, and he has no idea how to do it. He'll die if he tries. I've had my visions and seen it. You've got to stop him."

Kirk pointed toward a brown leather easy chair. "Sit down, Solea. You're far too upset about this magician's illusion. Let me get you some coffee."

Solea raised her voice. "I don't want coffee. I need you to stop Stanford from doing this."

Kirk stood straighter. "Me? How could I, even if I wanted to? I don't know the boy."

Solea took a long, deep breath, trying to regain her composure. "You have connections all over this city, Uncle. Surely you can make a call to someone who will keep Stanford from committing suicide. Get some of your police friends to arrest him."

"For what? You can't jail a man for being stupid."

A tear rolled down Solea's cheek and she wiped it away. "It can't be legal to do this silly stunt. Please, Uncle, you must do something."

Kirk tilted her head back with a finger. "Come now, Solea. Maybe the young man will regain his senses. Have you talked to him?"

"Yes. He told me he wouldn't do it, but this morning I found out he lied to me."

Kirk's lips formed a tight line. "You're not developing feelings for this young man, are you? I warned you that all magicians are cheats. I'm not surprised he lied to you."

Solea looked toward the floor and then up at Kirk. "I'm sorry, Uncle. I know you warned me, but I fell in love with him. That's why I don't want anything to happen to him."

Kirk's face reddened with anger. "Love him? Don't be foolish. You hardly know him. What's it been, less than two weeks? He's just another magician who would lie and cheat to get publicity. You can't possibly care about this boy. Our family comes before anything else. That's a lesson we all learn very young. Didn't your mother teach you that?"

"Of course she did, but I can't help the feelings I have. Stanford proposed to me last night." She fingered the necklace around her neck. "He bought this as a symbol of his love until he can afford to buy me an engagement ring. I agreed to marry him."

Kirk's eyes blazed and spittle flew from his lips. "What are you talking about? Marry him? This isn't possible. We manipulated him so you could get a job as his assistant and feed me information, not so you could fall in love. You have betrayed me. Is this the thanks I get for taking you in?"

"I would never betray family. Stanford is a good man. There's nothing he knows that would be of value to you. I would have told you if there were. Uncle, if you just meet him you'll understand why I love him."

Kirk stared, calmer now, his voice soothing. "Solea, listen to yourself. You're not making sense. How could you marry a boy who lied to you? Impossible. You must leave him. Allow the magician to kill himself with his foolish trick. There are more important things in life than this Stanford. I have so much to tell you about our plans. You're a big part of them."

Solea's voice rose. "I don't want to hear any more family stories."

Kirk's body stiffened. "Do not disrespect me. There is no discussion here. You must leave this magician."

Solea turned away. "You have no idea what I'm going through. You loved once. You must remember what it's like."

"There is no room for love when one is on a mission. Your mission was to get information that would be beneficial to me." He grabbed Solea's arm. "And you didn't."

Solea grimaced. "Uncle, you're hurting me."

Kirk's eyes narrowed. "Tell me one thing you learned." He dropped her arm and took several short, quick breaths.

Solea studied him for a few seconds. For the first time she feared the man. "Stanford does have this weird idea that Rabbi Weiss is really Houdini, but I don't know. It seems impossible to me. Stanford said Rabbi Weiss admitted it to him, but maybe he's lying to me again."

"You know how our family hates Houdini, yet you didn't tell me this. Didn't you think I'd be interested?"

"I wasn't sure it was true. If I thought it was important I would have told you."

"Ah. Not important." He clenched his fist and then loosened it. "You were to tell me everything, and I would decide what was useful." He shook his head. "I'm so disappointed in you, Solea. I had such big plans."

"You never told me about any plans. You're so secretive, Uncle. Rooms in the house that are always locked and strange men visiting at all hours. Maybe if you told me why it was important to get information from Stanford I would have known what I was looking for."

"It's too late now. I'd planned a special reward for your dedication to me."

"I don't understand."

"You see, I know Rabbi Weiss is really Houdini. I've known for several days. I had so hoped you'd prove your loyalty by giving me this information."

"Why is this so important to you? Houdini is no threat to anyone now. He's an old man who does good things for people."

"Again Solea you were thinking and again you were wrong."

"I'm sorry, Uncle. It's just . . ."

Kirk held up his hand. "No need to apologize. You can make up for it by telling me what you know about Houdini's plans for the Gleason show."

"Stanford told me he was going to be on. That's all I know."

"What time is he arriving at the theater? How is he going to get there?"

Solea shook her head rapidly. "Uncle, you're scaring me with all this talk about Houdini."

Kirk didn't respond.

"Won't you please help me save Stanford?"

"Of course. Doesn't your uncle always come through for you?" He jabbed a finger at her. "Has there ever been a time I failed you? Wait here while I make a phone call. If there's any way to stop Stanford from his foolishness, I will get it done."

Solea forced a smile. "Thank you."

Kirk walked into his bedroom and closed the door.

Solea paced, her mind preoccupied with Stanford. Hopefully, her uncle would be successful and Stanford would be stopped. But what was this obsession with Houdini about? She knew Uncle Anthony hated the man, but today he seemed deranged. He'd never gotten so angry with her. For an instant, she thought of the possibility that her uncle had been behind the attempt on Rabbi Weiss's life, but that seemed impossible. Her uncle had always been so gentle and kind. Until today.

She noticed that the door to his study was open a crack. "Uncle, you're getting absentminded." She raised her voice. "Your study is always locked."

There was no response from the other room. Kirk mumbled softly on the bedroom phone.

Solea had always been inquisitive as a young child and when she moved in with her uncle wondered about the mysterious things that went on in the house. She'd been curious about what he kept in his study and had fantasized what the room looked like. But he'd always kept it locked when she was in the house. She glanced toward the bedroom and then nervously pushed open the door.

The first thing she noticed was the human skulls—at least a dozen of them lining the bookshelves. Light filtered in from the lone window and shone directly on one. Solea cringed. Behind the skulls were books on séances, spiritualism, and religion.

Then her gaze took in the rest of the room.

Taped on the wall were several grainy pictures of Anthony Kirk, Sr., her uncle's father. He'd died many years ago, but Solea recognized him from a framed photo her uncle kept on the mantle. In front of the wall was a three-tiered small glass stand with several unlit candles. It seemed like a shrine and made her feel uneasy. Sure, her uncle idolized his father and talked incessantly about what a great man he was, but this tribute to him seemed bizarre.

She focused on a second wall. It was covered with Houdini playbills and posters. Slash marks were cut into many of them. Books and magazines about Houdini were on a table next to a make up kit.

But what was on the far wall made Solea gasp. Scrawled in large letters, in what appeared to be blood, were the words, "Houdini must die."

Solea's mind whirled. How could she have been so blind? She remembered her uncle's harsh words and hardened gaze when he'd spoken of Houdini earlier and his desire to know the details his appearance on the Gleason Show. Had she been so consumed with Stanford's safety, that she had missed the obvious?

As her horror grew, other things snapped into place. The contents of this room, her uncle's insistence she get a job with Stanford to get information, his strange behavior, and the shady Cuban man Solea had seen at the house several times all pointed to one conclusion. Then something else struck her. He had shown hatred for Stanford. What if he planned on killing him as well?

Fear jolted through her body. She had to get out of the house. She rushed out of the study and straight into the arms of her uncle.

"That room is off limits to you." His tone was harsh.

Solea took a step back, her breath coming in quick gasps, her heart galloping. She had to get away and warn Stanford about her fears. "I'm sorry, Uncle. The door was open and . . . ."

He gripped her wrist tightly with his right hand. "I ordered you not to enter that room when you first moved into my house."

Out of the corner of her eye, Solea noticed a cloth in his left hand. As he raised his arm toward her face, a bitter smell invaded her nostrils. Something was soaked into the cloth and he lifted it to her face.

Solea smashed her hand down on his arm, broke away from his grasp, and sprinted across the room. She collided with a chair, toppling it to the floor and sending a sharp pain up her leg. Kirk closed the space between them in seconds, grabbed her hair, and snapped her head back. Solea flailed her arms and kicked at him. A table fell on its side scattering books and magazines onto the rug.

Kirk wrapped his arm around her neck from behind, squeezing tightly.

Solea's hands balled into a fist, the tendons on her arms standing out in taut cords as she fought to break loose from Kirk's grasp. Her gaze frantically darted left and right in search of escape. A tear broke loose from her right eye and ran down her cheek. "You're hurting me."

"Your first betrayal was not telling me about Houdini." Kirk draped the cloth across her nose. "Your second betrayal was to fall in love with someone like Houdini. Marry him? I would never allow that. Don't you see what it would mean to the family? You have turned on us, and when someone betrays me I destroy them."

Solea's struggle slackened; her breathing became faint. Then her body slumped into his arms. He let it fall to the floor.

Kirk stood over her and glared down. "It's a shame you won't be able to see our nemesis killed on live television tonight. As for Stanford, Ramirez will see that his locks are tampered with and won't open. He will die on the same night as Houdini. That is true justice."

Kirk leaned down and tore the necklace from Solea's neck. He broke it apart and flung its pieces onto the floor. Then he went into the garage and came back with a large coil of rope. He wrapped it around Solea's prone body and tied her arms and legs tightly.

"You'll be out for hours, my dear." He tightened the last knot. "My father will tell me what to do about you just as he has guided me for the last forty years. I will be in contact with him shortly. Even if you regain consciousness you won't be able to break out of my special knots." He tugged on the rope. "These would hold even Houdini. You'll be here waiting for me when I get back."

He grabbed Solea under the shoulders and dragged her across the floor. He kicked open the door to a spare room and shoved her inside. Locking the door, he went out to his car, backed it out of the driveway, and sped up the street.

12
THIS TRICK IS MY DESTINY

Stanford paced the hotel room. He looked out the window toward the parking lot. The Mustang still hadn't returned. It was unlike Solea to go off without telling him, or at least leaving a note. He'd been out of the shower for thirty minutes and she still wasn't back. Was he becoming too possessive? She didn't have to tell him her every move.

His mind flashed back to last night. The jealousy he'd felt when she'd been with Sinatra, the joy and exhilaration when she agreed to marry him, and the happiness she displayed when he bought her the necklace. Their lovemaking had always been spectacular, but last night it reached a new level because they were committed to one another.

So where was she?

He thought about everything that had to be done before tonight's performance. Professionally this would be the greatest day of his life. He didn't like keeping a secret from Solea, but she'd left him no choice.

He gazed into the mirror and adjusted his shirt. He'd worn the white one with the puffy sleeves. He wanted to look like a true magician when he publicized tonight's Water Torture Cell Escape. This morning he planned on visiting various hotels and then he'd spend the afternoon rehearsing. The individual pieces of the trick he knew—the breaking out of handcuffs, how to get out of the chamber, and the importance of his breathing techniques. It was putting all of the pieces together underwater

99

that made the illusion so difficult. Yet, he was convinced he could pull it off, and the resulting publicity was worth the minimum risk.

There was a light tap on the door. When he opened it, Jim Calhoun stood in the hallway. His friend was dressed in a lightweight dark suit looking more like a successful businessman than the unemployed electrician that he was. With his military style haircut, horned-rimmed glasses, and average looks he was the type people barely noticed in a crowd. Stanford had used him as an audience plant several times to ask questions and produce props.

Stanford smiled. "You look like you're going to a funeral." He motioned the man inside.

Calhoun pointed to the shirt. "And you look like you're trying out for the part of a pirate in a movie." He tugged on his tie. "This morning we do publicity, and I wanted to look professional. Besides, how often do I get to wear my only suit?"

Stanford had met Calhoun at one of his shows in Miami a few weeks ago. He'd noticed the man sitting in the front row watching closely and nodding his head as if he knew all Stanford's secrets. At the time, Stanford didn't know Calhoun was a frustrated magician who, because of a car accident that permanently injured his knee, didn't have the agility to perform tricks. Afterwards they'd talk about the performance and despite Calhoun being fifteen years older than, Stanford, they were very much alike in ambition and temperament. Calhoun offered to help Stanford with publicity and moving props around the stage. Over the weeks, he'd grown to like the older man and gave him other jobs to do as well.

"So you didn't have any problem getting into Weiss's basement?" Stanford asked.

"Have I ever failed you? He kept his old locks and handcuffs in a chest downstairs just as you thought. He also has some exercise equipment down there. The old guy likes to keep in shape." Calhoun shook his head. "When I agreed to help you out I didn't think breaking and entering was going to be part of the deal."

"You did tell me you'd do anything. Who knows? With the publicity I get from this illusion I may hire you full time."

"You mean this could actually become a paying gig?" Calhoun

glanced around the room. "Where's Solea?"

"I'm not sure. She was gone when I got out of the shower, and she took the Mustang. I'm going to need you to drive me around today."

"Did she finally smarten up and walk out on you?"

"Hardly. As a matter of fact, we had a very special night last night. We saw Sinatra at the Fontainebleau and during the middle of the show I proposed to her on stage. We're getting married."

Calhoun grinned. "You proposed during Sinatra's show? You've got class, kid. Congratulations. I never thought The Great Stanford was the marrying type, but Solea is a beautiful woman. So the day after you propose, she disappears on you, huh?"

"She's probably out shopping. I told her I had a lot to do, so it surprises me a little. But, then again, who can understand women?"

"If you don't mind me asking, Boss, how are you planning on keeping this trick a secret from Solea? It doesn't seem like a very good way to start a relationship."

"So far I've managed to do it. It shouldn't be that big a deal to her. She's afraid something will happen to me. Once the trick is over and she sees all the accolades I get, she'll be glad I did it. I told her I'm having dinner with friends tonight and I'd meet her later."

"When she finds out, I think you're going to see a little of that Spanish temper." Calhoun looked away for an instant. "I've got some concerns about the trick."

"Now you sound like Solea. What concerns?"

"I checked some of the handcuffs and chains I got from Houdini. They're old and rusty. We should replace them with new ones. There's too much of a chance something could go wrong."

Stanford pushed his hand through his hair. "That's out of the question. Part of the legend I want to grow from my escape tonight will be that I used Houdini's original equipment. I'll have it verified by experts right after the performance. It's an essential part of the publicity I want to create. That's why I had you steal them. We'll work on them this afternoon. A little grease and oil should have them working like new."

"I already tried that, but they still don't function easily. The stunt is hard enough. Let's not make it more difficult. Do you have a back up plan if things go wrong when you're underwater?"

"Everything will go smoothly." He tapped his chest with his fist. "Performing this trick is my destiny. I've never been so sure of anything in my life. I will not be defeated. Now, let's go. I've got a lot to get done before tonight's performance. Let's emphasize the uncertainty of my surviving the trick today. People like danger, and it will attract more spectators."

"It *is* dangerous, Boss. I hope you know what you're doing."

"Why do so many people doubt me?"

RABBI WEISS'S BASEMENT – MIAMI BEACH

The thudding sounds echoed through the finished basement. Rabbi Weiss pounded the large leather punching bag that hung from the metal stand. He wore black sweatpants, a white tee shirt, and brown boxing gloves. Perspiration glistened on his face. The rubber soles of his sneakers squeaked on the cement floor. His body moved quickly from side to side as he put his full weight behind each jab.

He grunted each time he hit the bag, feeling pain in his shoulders and back. He'd noticed his regular workouts had been getting harder recently. But still, he was in pretty good shape for a man his age. He hit the target high and then low. He stopped and stared at the swaying bag. He felt exhausted, but had to continue. There was no telling what danger he'd face shortly. As he'd done his entire life he needed to be sure he had the best chance to succeed. He took a step back and with renewed energy struck the bag with such force it lifted off its stand and crashed to the floor.

13

THE CASSADAGA SPIRITUALIST

Anthony Kirk slowly drove his 1966 black Lincoln Continental along the main street of Cassadaga. The day was overcast, with a light drizzle glistening on the downtown street. He passed the Spanish Mission style Cassadaga Hotel, the shoebox sized post office, and a small bookstore, the only establishments in the center of town.

Cassadaga was known as the psychic center of the world. Visitors had flocked there for over a hundred years to gain insight, understanding, and guidance from the spiritual world. The town was founded by trance medium George P. Colby, who set up the Southern Cassadaga Spiritualism Camp. According to legend, Colby's spiritual guide, Seneca, instructed him to establish a spiritual community on this spot because of its ethereal vibrations, which allowed readings between spiritualists and clients to be conducted with the utmost clarity.

Anthony Kirk loved this town. The people of Cassadaga were open and compassionate, and believed everyone was a little psychic. Kirk's father had studied in the Cassadaga Spiritualist Camp for ten years to become one of the best spiritualists in the country. As an only child, Anthony spent his childhood in this small hamlet playing in the surrounding forest with imaginary friends to make up for the lack of kids in the neighborhood his own age. His mother had home schooled him, but he always felt he hadn't missed anything by not going to public schools. He'd learned the important things: reading, writing, thinking, and loyalty to family right by his mother's side.

His father had always been larger than life to him. His earliest memories were of how his father had swept him up into his lap, which was the best place to be because it came with a pair of protective arms. He was so proud when he realized his father was famous; people would come from far away to listen to his words and heed his wisdom. One of his visitors had been Houdini trying to contact his dead mother, and then the magician had turned on his father calling him a con man and a charlatan. He'd singled him out by name and destroyed the man with a vicious vendetta. Kirk had watched his father dwindle, as if diminishing in size right before his eyes, lose hope, and die of a broken heart due to the ridicule some heaped on him because of Houdini's words.

Tonight his father's death would be avenged.

He stopped in front of a two-story white house with thin Doric columns and a white picket railing enclosing the porch. A brown wooden sign on the side said, in fading black letters, "The Cassadaga Spiritualist, Adeline Kirk on duty." The words were surrounded by a crystal ball. He loved that logo. It always made him feel proud when he looked at the sign and saw his mother's name.

Kirk remembered how quiet the town was when he was growing up, and today was no different. There were no cars on the street, few pedestrians walking, and not a playing child in sight. Quiet was the word most people used to describe the town.

He got out of the car, walked up the rickety front steps, and entered a large room lit by flickering candles. The room was small and square, the only furniture being a large oval table surrounded by four wooden chairs in the center of the room and a couple of tiny shelves against the wall. A long back curtain shielded the adjoining rooms. The air smelled of incense and stale tobacco.

"Mother?" Kirk yelled.

The shuffling of dragging feet came from the back room, and then a heavyset woman in her late seventies pushed through the curtains into the main room. Her long, tangled gray hair flowed to her waist. Her face was wrinkled and covered with thick makeup. She wore a flowing black dress with several bracelets on her right wrist and colorful rings on each finger.

Her bracelets jangled as she reached out to her son. "I

expected you sooner. This is a special day for the Kirk family. You father has much he wants to tell you."

Kirk hugged his mother for a brief moment. Affection was not something either one displayed, although they loved each other deeply. "I was delayed at home, but that's been taken care of." He smiled. "Tonight what we've wanted for so long will finally happen. No more failures. I can guarantee it."

Mother Kirk's posture straightened, and she brushed a strand of gray hair behind her ear. With that gesture, the years seemed to drop off her before his eyes. It was as if the idea of revenge had given her a quick shot of youth.

"You've always been a wonderful son. I knew when you were very young that I'd never have to worry about you."

"You and Father have always taken care of me."

Mother Kirk lit a few more candles, but the room was still dim. "You won't have me around much longer I'm afraid, but you'll do great things without me. You've always been a fighter. I remember when you were four years old and you fell against that table." She pointed toward the oval table. "I heard the crash and came rushing into the room. There was blood everywhere and the cut was so deep it required stitches. Do you know what you did?"

Kirk had heard this story many times, but he played along because his mother took such joy in telling it.

"I imagine I cried and screamed quite a bit."

"No, Anthony. When I arrived, you were hitting the table. Pounding it as if it had attacked you. I knew then that I'd never have to worry about you. That no matter what happened you'd never be a quitter. It was such a shock to find out that Houdini was still alive after we thought him dead all these years, but I knew you'd take care of him and that he would pay the price for what he put us through. Tell me, how do you plan to do it?"

Kirk's posture stiffened, a look of pride on his face. "It will be dramatic, Mother. He'll be killed in front of a live television audience on the Jackie Gleason show tonight. Millions will see him take his final breath. Father will be so proud. And the wonderful thing is you'll be able to watch and see it done. The plan couldn't work out any better."

"I hope you have someone smarter than the last two you hired to kill Houdini."

"That was a mistake. I realize that now. I should have consulted with Father before I sent them out. This time I will kill Houdini. No one else has the determination to get it done. I will avenge my father's death."

Mother Kirk's eyes narrowed, and she touched her son's shoulder. "But how will you escape? This sounds dangerous for you."

Kirk raised a hand as if waving off her objections. "I have a foolproof way to get away. Don't worry about that. Just make sure you're watching so you can enjoy the show. That will make the killing that much sweeter for me."

Mother Kirk gave a half smile. "Your plan is brilliant. He must suffer the way he made us suffer. You are a genius and will make a great president."

"Thank you, Mother, but we do have one small problem. Solea."

"What's the girl done now? I never liked her. I couldn't figure out why you agreed to take her in or why you developed such an interest in her."

"I thought she could help us, but I was wrong. She has betrayed our family. She withheld information about Houdini, but worse she plans to marry a magician. Someone who talked to Houdini. There's no telling what kind of lies the magician told him. He could be a problem as well."

"Marry a magician? Like Houdini? Surely she understands family loyalty and our hatred for all magicians."

"No, Mother, she didn't. I went out of my way to shield her from the truth until the time was right. After she'd given me what I needed to know, then I planned to tell her, assuming she'd understand." He looked away for an instant. "Maybe I was wrong. Maybe if I'd told her everything right away she would have acted differently."

"This is no time to be weak." Anger filled the woman's voice. "Your father will tell us what to do about Solea, the same way he has guided us for many years. Where is she now?"

"Under my control and not able to escape until we decide what to do with her. I will do with her whatever Father instructs."

"And what of this young magician? If he talked to Houdini, he could be a problem as well."

"He will be taken care of. The fool is planning on performing Houdini's Water Torture Cell Escape tonight. That's proof he has been discussing things with the magician. I've made the necessary phone call to ensure his death. The locks he uses to secure himself will not open and he will drown. It will appear like an accident."

"Houdini's death was to appear like an accident forty years ago, and those men failed us."

"It will not happen this time. Everything will go according to plan."

"I trust you, son, and when the Kirk name is well known again, people will flock here to have the President's mother contact their dead relatives. Your father predicted I would become the world's greatest psychic, and so it shall be."

"I need to talk to Father. I want to make sure there will be no last minute complications to my plan."

"Would you like me to contact him now?"

"Please, Mother. Tonight I need his guidance and blessing more than ever. I was so angry, I almost killed Solea. I must know if that's the best thing to do with her. I don't want to upset our ancestors. Maybe she can be saved and be of some use to us. Father will know."

"I don't see how Solea can be helpful, but Father will advise you."

Kirk sat in one of the folding chairs. Mother Kirk blew out a few candles and then sat next to him at the oval table. She took his hand and closed her eyes. A gust of wind blew the curtains and a tree branch knocked against the side of the house. For several seconds those were the only sounds in the room.

"Father," Mother Kirk said, "today is the day we've all waited for. It will mark the end of the curse of Houdini. Let us know that everything will go as planned."

Moments passed. A shutter banged on the window and the oval table moved slightly, causing a tapping on the floor, slowly at first and then faster. A wisp of fog seeped into the room from the window, casting eerie flickering shadows on the wall.

"My son." Mother's Kirk's voice lowered, sounding much like her husband. "You have always made me proud, but tonight you will outdo yourself. It will be a remarkable one for the Kirk family. Go with my blessing and perform as only a true Kirk is able to."

Kirk sat very still, his eyes shut, his hand squeezing his mother's.

"I'm doing this for our family, but most of all to honor you. Your blessing is so important to me, but I need to know that everything will go smoothly."

Silence. Then the table shook again.

Mother Kirk leaned toward her son, and he could smell her foul breath. "I'm losing him," she said.

The walls rattled and the wisps of fog receded around the window.

"Get him back," Kirk said. "Today of all days I need his guidance."

Mother Kirk's voice lowered again. "Houdini will die tonight just as we want. You will survive and go on to greater fame. Do not change one detail of your plan. Follow through and America will become a better place for all to live."

"What about Solea, Father?"

"Solea has betrayed us. Do not hesitate to kill her. She cannot be trusted. You must do it quickly."

Mother Kirk slumped in the chair, her arms falling limp. Her eyes flickered for a moment and then they opened wide. She took a long breath, as if the ordeal had exhausted her. "Your father has spoken. You must do as he says and quickly. It's part of the family legacy."

"Haven't I always done as Father asked?"

Mother Kirk got up and staggered slightly.

Kirk jumped to his feet, rushed to her side, and grabbed her elbow. "Mother? Are you all right?"

She nodded. "You have always been a good son. I am tired now. Communicating with your father has been getting more difficult lately. I don't know how much longer you will have me."

"Don't talk like that, Mother. You'll live a long life. You must see your only child rise to fame and glory."

Mother Kirk stared into his eyes, but her gaze was unfocused. "Go now and do as your father wishes."

Kirk hugged his mother for a long moment. "I will kill Solea first and then go to the theater and take care of Houdini. The young magician will be dead by then. Halloween of 1966 will be a great day for the Kirk Family. My father has spoken."

"God speed, son."

As Kirk left, he had a premonition that this would be the last time he'd see his mother alive.

14

SOLEA'S EYES FLICKERED

ANTHONY KIRK'S BEACH HOUSE – MIAMI BEACH

Solea's eyes flickered open. The room spun, and then slowly came into focus. Her head hurt, her wrists ached, and her thoughts were foggy, as if everything were moving in slow motion. For a moment, she didn't know where she was.

Then her mind cleared and it all came back to her: arriving at the house, her uncle's irrational words, the unlocked study door, the bloody threat to Houdini, and the acidic odor of the cloth that covered her nose. Sunlight filtered around the edges of a heavy shaded window, but she had no idea how long she'd been out.

She tugged on the ropes, vaguely remembering something her uncle said about Stanford. Rolling on her side, she tried to yank her wrists wider apart, but the harder she struggled the tighter the knots became.

"Help," she yelled. "Please. Someone. Anyone."

A jolt of terror passed through her body. Her uncle's house was isolated. No one could hear her cries. The pounding surf would deafen even people strolling on the beach.

She tried to sit up, but fell flat. Rolling on her side, she glanced around the room searching for a way to escape. She gasped. A skeleton, its bones smeared with blood, was mounted on a coat rack, the name Houdini printed on a cardboard sign and attached to the skull. In front of a draped window, several dead flamingos were stacked in a wooden create. Lying in front of the crate was a black clay doll with a sewing needle protruding from its neck. The floor was littered with yellowing magazines and newspapers. The room smelled of decay.

Plastered on the walls were cut out news articles from the 1920s noting Houdini's defamation of Spiritualists. Many were covered with blood.

The room terrified her. *What kind of curse did you try to put on Houdini, Uncle?* Solea thought. How could she not have seen what a madman he was?

She yanked on the rope again and felt it dig into her wrists. Staring at the ceiling, she took several short, quick breaths. She had to relax and focus. She'd never get out of here if she panicked.

Then a thought entered her mind and she gazed upward. "God," she said aloud. "You've given me visions before. People ridiculed me, but I always realized what a gift they were. There were so many times you managed to help me. Help me now. Please. My uncle will kill Stanford and Houdini unless I act. Give me a sign. Let me know you're here."

She listened, not sure what to expect. Would God talk to her? Would her ropes suddenly loosen? Would Stanford miraculously appear and rescue her. The only sound was the whooshing of the wind through the trees outside.

She closed her eyes. "Maybe you've given me powers I don't know about, and if I concentrate you will help me." She raised her voice. "Stanford, I am here. Please help me. Houdini. I need help. Can anyone hear me? I can't escape on my own. Come to me. Come to me, now."

She heard the sound of a creaking floorboard in the next room. Solea stiffened and waited for the door to burst open. Was it her uncle? Did he plan to kill her? There was silence for several long seconds. She let out a stuttering breath. Maybe it was the normal shifting of an older house.

She lay quietly, staring upward. Her breathing returned to normal, but her head throbbed. She couldn't let her uncle defeat her. Defeat them. She had to fight with everything she had. There must be a way to escape.

A gust of wind rattled the window, startling her. Hazy wisps of fog seeped through the walls and surrounded her. Faint images entered her consciousness, too dim to make out. Her headache worsened, and she scrunched her eyes for an instant to ease the pain. The images became clearer, more distinct. A room—small, an oval table. An older woman with tangled, gray hair and a long flowing black dress was seated on a folding chair. She recognized Adeline Kirk from family pictures. Then a second figure came into focus. The woman held Uncle Anthony's hand. In the flickering candlelight of the room, they appeared translucent and ghost-like.

Suddenly Solea felt a presence around her. She craned her neck. "Who's in the room?" Silence, but she was sure she wasn't alone. Then Anthony Kirk Sr.'s face appeared before her in a grainy image. His features faded in and out of focus, yet for some reason she was sure he was real.

"This is crazy," Solea said. "You're dead. Is this vision only in my mind? Am I going insane?"

The skeleton behind her rattled, and a gust of wind fluttered the newspapers and magazines on the floor.

A voice hovered over Solea and seemed to fill every inch of the room. It was loud and echoed off the walls. "You've always had visions, even as a child. Your mother told me of them. I had very high hopes for you. I thought you could become one of us. You've proved not to be worthy."

Solea shivered. "How? I don't understand."

The image floated up and disappeared from Solea's sight. "You will die, Solea. Accept it. Do not fight us. There's no way you can win."

Solea strained against the ropes. "No, I will not give up. I love Stanford, and I will save him."

The image roared loudly, then came back into view a few inches from Solea's face. "And that love will kill the both of you."

"No," she screamed.

The ghost-like fog roared again, then circled around the room as it floated to the ceiling. A moment later- it was gone, and the room was filled with a deadly quiet.

Solea's shoulders slumped. Was she hallucinating? Was this just her imagination? A shadowy image appeared inches from her face and jolted her. Mother Kirk was seated alone at the oval table. In a low voice she said, "Solea must die. Solea must die." Her eyes were wide, her hair shooting wildly in the air. Then the skin from the woman's face shriveled and dripped from her bones, covering the table with a gooey, sticky pale sheen. Adeline Kirk's skeleton smiled.

Solea's breath came in short bursts and sweat dripped down her forehead. She closed her eyes. Another vision, and this one made her gasp. A translucent image of Solea floated in the air above as if coming fully formed out of her body. But it wasn't her. It resembled her, but the image was nude and the head, three times normal size.

"Am I going crazy? God, please don't forsake me."

The image circled and swooped overhead. Then it floated out of the room, leaving Solea alone in the stillness.

Solea's ghost-like image broke through the ceiling of the house and moved out onto the beach. It burrowed into the sand, disappeared, and came out further up the beach. She could see all this in her mind as if it were really happening.

In the distance, an older man whistled and tossed rocks into the water. He looked up as the wispy fog got closer and a look of confusion crossed his face. He studied the vision and shook his head, as if not believing what he had seen. Then he stooped, picked up another rock, and continued to walk along the beach.

Solea lay still, her eyes open, her gaze vacant, her breathing shallow. The floor of the room shook slightly. An instant later the ghost-like image whooshed in through the wall and entered her body. Her eyes flickered and gradually closed. She felt herself losing consciousness and struggled to keep her eyes open. *Fight*, she said to herself. *Do not give up*.

Suddenly she tensed, alerted to a different sound—scratching against the house, like an animal trying to enter.

Her uncle?

She tugged on the ropes in a last effort to break free.

There it was again. Scraping, as if something were rubbing against the wall. Then wood shattered and footsteps tapped across the floor.

"Here," Solea yelled. "Help me. Please."

The doorknob shook. Solea's eyes widened and she held her breath. A thump against the wood, and then a loud crash. The door shattered, popped back, and banged into the wall creating a narrow crack.

Solea recognized the old man on the beach.

He rushed toward her. "Jesus, lady. Are you all right?"

Solea nodded, wondering how he'd known where she was and why he'd broken into the house.

He bent over her and yanked on the rope. "Who tied these knots? Even Houdini couldn't break out of these."

"In the kitchen," Solea said. "A knife."

The man disappeared for a few moments and came back carrying a large knife. He sliced the rope and began to unwrap it from her arms and legs. "What happened?"

Solea slipped out of the cut rope, her mind focused on what to do next. She got to her feet and flexed her muscles, still feeling the rope burns on her wrist.

"Do you have some kind of strange power?" the man asked.

"What do you mean?"

"I saw your image on the beach." The man squinted. "Yeah, it was you all right. It was like a fog hovering in the air, floating every which way. I figured it was just an old man's mind playing tricks, but it seemed so real. After I walked up a ways, I knew I had to come back, that I'd seen that vision for a reason. I looked in the window, saw the table and chair overturned, and a voice told me to go inside, that someone was in trouble. It was the weirdest thing that's ever happened to me. This has to be a dream."

Solea stared upward. "Thank you, God." She refocused on the stranger. "It's not a dream. I reached out to you with my mind. It was an act of God."

The old man stood very still. "I don't know what it was or how you did it, but you got me here."

"This is something you must never mention. Too many people would be frightened of me if they knew the real story. Promise me."

"Don't worry about me mentioning it. I don't want anyone to think I'm nuts." He looked around the room as if seeing it for the first time. "Jesus. What kind of place is this?"

"The home of a madman," Solea said quietly.

The old man stared at her for an instant. "We should get you to a hospital to be checked out."

"What time is it?"

He glanced at his watch. "Almost seven. Why?"

Solea's legs shook, and she wobbled toward the door. The effects of whatever her uncle had given her still lingered, making her thoughts unfocused and her movements slow. There was still time. There had to be.

"I have to get to the pier. I just hope I'm not too late."

The old man touched her arm to steady her. "You're in no condition to go anywhere. You can hardly walk. And your wrists are all covered with blood. Let me get you some help before you pass out."

"But I must. God will look after me."

15

ONE CLEAR SHOT

Kirk stopped his Lincoln Town Car in his driveway with a stomp on the brakes. He slammed his fist on the steering wheel. The Mustang was gone. How could the bitch have escaped? He'd drugged her, tied her tightly using his special knots, and locked her up. Someone had to have helped her, but who had known where she was?

He closed his car door hard and stomped up the front walk. His gaze darted left and right searching, hoping he'd see her in the distance. He didn't need this complication. His temple throbbed as he focused on what this meant for his plans, and he tried to wipe the thought out of his mind as he rushed inside. The door to his office was splintered and he noted the sliding glass door to the beach was shattered.

Could Stanford have rescued her? Or possibly Houdini?

It took a moment for him to realize that the loud scream piercing the silent house was coming from his throat. Just the thought of Houdini in his home nauseated him.

He gripped the living room couch and took several long breaths trying to calm down. He couldn't be rattled. He had too much to do. What did Solea know anyway? She couldn't possibly be aware of his plot, and even if by some miracle she figured it out, there was no way she could stop him. His father had told him tonight's events would be successful.

He glanced at his watch. He had an hour to get to the theater and couldn't take the time to look for her or worry about what she was doing. He'd deal with her later in the cold, brutal way that was required for an act of betrayal. He felt better realizing that at that moment Stanford was preparing to perform the Water Cell Torture Escape. It wouldn't be long until the young magician was dead.

He walked into his bedroom and sat in a chair in front of the mirror. He examined his face, the bags under his eyes and the strained expression. Opening the small box on the table he took out his make up and applied it liberally, darkening his skin. Then he added latex to his cheeks so they appeared fuller. He worked on his nose, giving it an angular appearance. Removing his shirt, he added padding and then slipped it back on. He put his gray sport jacket on and admired his reflection. Even his own mother wouldn't recognize him.

He left the bedroom and went to the desk in his study. Opening a drawer, he took out his gun and examined it closely. It was loaded and ready to use. He ran his finger along the barrel and enjoyed the jolt of power the weapon gave him. He shoved it into his jacket pocket.

He had one more thing to do before leaving for the theater.

Walking through the house and into his office, he knelt in front of the shrine he'd built in honor of his father. The photos and press clippings always made him proud to be the son of such a great man. He lit a few candles and gazed at the large photo in the center. "I trust you, Father. Things have started to go wrong, but your words telling me that Houdini will die tonight and I will survive still ring in my ears. Your death will be avenged." He picked a ticket up and waved it in the air as if his father would be able to see it. "A front row seat to the Gleason show. One clear shot to the stage and the magician's life will be over. I will escape in the confusion, pulling off my disguise as I run. The police will be looking for a jowly heavy man, not Anthony Kirk. Your greatest prophecy was that I would become President. Tonight I will take a giant step toward that goal. The Kirk name will live forever in glory. It's what we both wanted."

He touched his father's picture and bowed his head in prayer. A few minutes later, he left the house knowing that tonight would be the greatest of his life.

RABBI WEISS'S STUDY – MIAMI BEACH

Rabbi Weiss adjusted his tuxedo jacket and stared at his reflection in the mirror. He'd spent the last hour shaving his beard. The deep wrinkles on his face had been covered for years, and he hardly recognized the man staring back at him. He tapped his stomach. He hadn't gained a pound in forty years and although he couldn't work out the way he once did, he kept in shape by daily walking, working out in his basement gym, and watching what he ate. Still, he'd noticed his stamina slipping the past few years. Even the great Houdini could not escape time.

He turned sideways to examine his profile. It had been a long time since he'd felt so exhilarated. He took a pair of handcuffs off his desk, slipped them on, and within seconds removed them. He smiled and his mind flashed back to tricks he'd performed during his earlier days—The Metamorphosis had always been his favorite. He remembered Bess and how much she enjoyed the illusion. The rapid substitution of one person for another inside a roped and locked box always amazed the crowd. It required agility and pinpoint timing, but those had always been his strengths. Then there were the straitjacket escapes, the vanishing elephant, the sewing needle illusion, and the numerous times he'd broken out of local jails. Sure, there'd been a few failures and during his younger days he'd obsess on them, but as he grew older, he realized failure was just another part of life.

The real trick had always been keeping his name at the top of any headlining bill, and that required perfecting new and better tricks. It had been a challenge, but he'd managed to do it.

There was a light tap on the door and then Karen Bonanno entered the study. Her gray hair was tied back in a bun, and the long black dress she wore made her look matronly and older than her fifty plus years. Her mother, Rose, had been Houdini's housekeeper in 1926. Karen was one of the few people aware of Weiss's secret identity and no one had been more loyal to him over the years.

Her eyes widened. "I hardly recognized you. My goodness, you look the same as you did forty years ago."

Weiss rubbed his cheek. "Thank you, Karen, but I'm afraid age has caught up with me. If I appeared on the show with a long beard, the viewers might not believe I was Houdini."

Karen's expression hardened as she placed a cup of tea on his desk. "I thought you might like this."

Weiss smiled. "Are you going to make one last attempt to talk me out of going on the Gleason show tonight?"

"I just want to make sure you're aware of what this decision means."

He picked up the cup. "Oh, I am, and I've never been surer of anything in my life." He took a sip of tea, and then put the cup back on the desk, hoping his words sounded more confident than he felt at that moment. "I've missed show business, Karen. There's something about a cheering crowd that always excited me. Bess loved it, too. She'd want me to do this. Your mother would have encouraged me as well. She was a great woman."

"My mother would have done a better job talking you out of this. I've been with you a lot of years and you've become like a father to me. I don't want anything to happen to you."

Weiss smiled and put a hand on her shoulder. "And you're like a daughter to me. Your friendship and loyalty are beyond question. I hope over the years I've made your life a little better. You may not agree with my decision, but allow me to do what I must with dignity. Your mother would have."

Karen glanced out the window for a moment, then refocused on Weiss. "I know how stubborn you can be, but this is dangerous. Suppose another attempt is made on your life?"

"I expect there might be, but certainly not on live television. That would be foolhardy, and the man behind the attempts on my life is not a fool."

"You know who it is?"

"Oh, I've known for many years. When he died I thought I was safe, but now I realize his son is responsible."

"Go to the police."

"The only proof I have is my certainty." Weiss shrugged. "If I am to die, so be it. I have lived a full life and have known some wonderful people. During the last forty years, I've made a difference in a lot of lives. How many can say that? It's time for me to be true to what I was really brought into this world to do?—to perform magic."

Karen studied him for a few seconds. "I know you too well, Rabbi. There's more to your going on the show tonight than just your desire to be in the spotlight again. What aren't you telling me?"

"Tonight I intend to expose the man who tried to kill me, Karen. His identity will surprise many. I know it's a dangerous thing, but I've sat back for too long. If something happens to me, the temple will be rebuilt and another rabbi will be found. No one is irreplaceable. The world moves on."

"What are you talking about? Of course the temple will find another leader, but no one did more to help the people of Miami than you did. Saving and caring for others was your true calling. I implore you not to do this."

"It's too late for that. I've given Gleason my word. And besides, too many know my true identity. I could be killed at any time. How could I protect against it? Destroying the temple was more than I could bear. This has got to be stopped, and doing the Gleason show may just save my life."

"Bess would have been strongly against this."

"I disagree. Bess would have understood the importance of my doing the performance. I'll show the audience what true magic is and then I'll expose the person behind the recent attempts on my life—and I'll do it all as only Houdini would." He smiled. "With a dramatic flare."

"Oh, Rabbi . . ."

Weiss shook his head. "Nothing you say will talk me out of it. Don't you see that I can't let this opportunity pass? It may never come again."

"I'm worried about you."

Weiss smiled again. "I'll be fine. I may be an old man, but I still have the instinct to survive. You must trust me on this."

Karen closed the door as she left. Weiss waited a few seconds and then pushed on a bookcase behind him. It slid open, revealing a set of stairs going down into the basement. This part of the cellar was separated from the rest by a cement wall he'd built himself. It was the room he went to when he wanted to be alone with his past.

A large black trunk was on the floor. Playbills and old Houdini posters filled every inch of wall space. A framed photo of Bess was on a small table.

"Bess," Weiss said, "whatever happens tonight, please know I've always loved you. If there is an afterlife I could be joining you shortly."

Weiss flipped open the trunk. He took out a pair of

handcuffs and an old axe. His eyes widened, and he fumbled inside frantically searching, pulling out locks and chains. Someone had been in his trunk. He glanced at the door leading out to the backyard and noticed that it had been forced open. Then he realized what was missing. *That fool,* he thought. *Stanford has taken my escape chains and locks. He's going to perform the Water Torture Cell Escape tonight. It will cost him his life.* He rushed up the stairs and out of his study.

"Karen," he yelled. "Call Gleason. Tell him I will definitely make the show before it's over. Tell him I may be late. I have to stop a fool from killing himself first. I just hope I'm not too late."

JACKIE GLEASON THEATER – MIAMI BEACH

Kirk parked his car in a lot near the theater. He stared at his reflection in the mirror and didn't recognize himself. His heart pounded as he watched people walking along the street. He reached inside his jacket and touched the gun to calm himself. This was the night he'd dreamed of all his life. There would be no mistakes.

He got out of the Lincoln. The night was cool and cloud free. He glanced toward the sky and wondered if at that moment his father was looking down on him. The thought relaxed him.

He moved quickly, not looking right or left, his mind focused, hardly aware of the crowd milling around him. He could sense their excitement and hear their loud voices, but he tried to block it out. Little did they know they'd be the witness to a momentous event.

He stopped in front of the theater and glanced up at the marquee. Big bold letters announced the Gleason show. Entering the lobby, he gave his ticket to the man at the entrance.

"Enjoy the show," he said.

Kirk smiled and moved forward. The man had no idea the irony of his words and the chaos that would occur shortly after the show started. He looked upward in a final prayer to his father.

An usher studied his ticket. "Front row, sir." The confusion was evident on his face, probably wondering how this bizarre looking man had gotten such a good seat.

He walked slowly down the aisle, recognizing a few people in the audience, and sat in his seat. He noted the position of the exits and knew he'd have no trouble escaping in the confusion. So far, everything had gone according to his careful plan.

A thick, red velvet curtain blocked the stage. He slipped his hand inside his sport jacket and touched his gun one more time for reassurance. More people entered the theater and the seats around him filled slowly. He checked his watch. Ten minutes until showtime. He wondered what was going on over at Hallover Pier.

16
SABOTAGED HIS LOCK?

WOLFIE'S DELI – MIAMI BEACH – THE LARRY KING SHOW

"Our guest tonight is Johnny Carson who appears nightly on The Tonight Show from New York City. What brings you to town, Johnny?"

"Gleason invited me to come back stage during his show tonight. How could I pass up an invitation like that?"

"The buzz in this town about Houdini is amazing. Any idea what Gleason has planned?"

"Jackie's not talking, and believe me I tried to get it out of him. My guess would be he'll have Houdini play Ralph Kramden, someone will lock Ralph in a bus, and then he'll escape. Either that or Ed gets trapped in the sewer and Houdini saves him."

King laughed. "Some people are saying Gleason will conduct a séance and contact Houdini while others feel Houdini never died and is actually going to be on the show tonight. If that's the case, maybe you could get him on The Tonight Show."

"Sure, if you're watching, Harry, I'll give you the whole hour. Just think of what you could do in New York City. How about being handcuffed and tossed into the Hudson River? Nah. You'd probably get out of the restraints, but the pollution would kill you. I've got an idea. You could hang over the side of the NBC building in a straitjacket next to Ed McMahon. Ed would be free within ten minutes because that's the longest he can go without a drink. Houdini could learn something from Ed."

"I don't know about you, Johnny, but I've had this spooky feeling all day just anticipating tonight's show. One of the things

123

I'm sure of is the whole nation will be watching. There's another story going on in town as well. What do you think of this Stanford kid claiming to be Houdini's protégé? He's been going all over town claiming that someday he'll be better known than Houdini." King glanced at his watch. "He's supposed to be performing Houdini's Water Torture Cell Escape right about now."

"I don't know if he's Houdini's protégé or not, but the kid's got guts. I wouldn't want to be chained in a box and tossed into the ocean. That trick killed Houdini. If Stanford comes out of this alive he's got an open invitation to appear on The Tonight Show."

HALLOVER PIER – MIAMI BEACH

Rabbi Weiss double parked his car on the street and jumped out. A large crowd packed the pier, and he craned his neck to see over them. Many wore Halloween costumes and several had Houdini masks on. There seemed to be almost a carnival atmosphere.

"Has the magician started his illusion yet?" Weiss asked a man a few inches in front of him.

"Not yet. They're putting him in the box now."

Weiss's mind whirled. How could he stop Stanford? With all the people waiting to see his performance, if the magician backed out, it would be humiliating. Stanford was proud and impetuous. It would be difficult to talk him out of it. *Take it one step at a time,* Weiss told himself. *Get the magician's attention and the right words will come.*

He noticed film trucks from NBC-WCKT and CBS-WTVJ parked off to the side. A reporter from radio station WINZ gripped a microphone and stared nervously over her shoulder.

Weiss tried to push through the crowd but found an unyielding mass. "I'm Rabbi Weiss. Please let me though. This must be stopped." His voice was barely audible above the noise, and he couldn't get beyond the tightly packed throng.

A man he knew didn't recognize him. "Nice try, but you're not Rabbi Weiss. I don't think you'd be able to get up front even if you were. This group has been staking out spaces for hours to get a glimpse of this crazy man."

"But I must."

Out of the corner of his eye, he spotted Solea pulling on a woman's shoulder and pleading to be let through. He moved toward her. Her eyes locked on his, but he knew she thought he was a stranger.

"It's Rabbi Weiss, Solea. I've shaved my beard."

A look of recognition crossed her face. "Please, you must stop him. He's going to die."

Weiss noticed the red marks on her neck and pointed. "What happened to you?"

"It's my uncle. He attacked me and tied me up." She grabbed Weiss's wrists. "He's sabotaged Stanford's locks. He was behind the attempt on your life at the theater."

Weiss glanced toward the water. "Sabotaged his locks? Are you sure?"

"He thought I had passed out, but I heard his every word. We have to warn Stanford."

"Is your uncle Anthony Kirk?"

Solea's eyes widened. "You know him?"

"His father tried to kill me forty years ago. I suspected his son was behind this, but I had no proof until now."

"Tried to kill you? Then you really are Houdini."

Weiss studied her. He could hear the love for Stanford in her words. His mind flashed back to Bess, the only woman he'd ever loved, and how intense it had been. He would have done anything for her. In that instant he knew, he had to save Stanford.

"Yes," Weiss said quietly. "I am. We must move quickly. There's still time to stop this."

A loud splash and the throng of people pushed closer to the pier, roaring as they moved. Weiss closed his eyes. Why hadn't he moved faster?

"Listen to them," Solea said. "They want blood. If Stanford dies, none of them would care. It would give them something else to talk about over dinner tonight."

Weiss stared in the direction of the pier, his heart hammering, not sure what to do. Maybe by some miracle Stanford would break free and survive.

Solea grabbed Weiss's shirt. "How deep is the water here?"

"Over fifty feet," he said quietly.

Solea looked skyward. "Oh, God. Please help him." Her eyes filled with tears. "Don't let him die." She turned to Weiss. "There must be something we can do. Isn't there a way to get him out of there? Can't they pull the cell out of the water?"

Weiss knew there wasn't time, and as the seconds passed, his fear grew. In his prime he could hold his breath for over three minutes, but that had been with years of practice in his bathtub in his New York City home. Stanford was young, but if he panicked he wouldn't last that long. Stanford had only one chance. Weiss knew what he had to do.

Solea tried to separate the crowd. "I must go to him. I can't let him die."

Weiss walked away from her and circled to the rear of the crowd to a part of the pier less crowded. He leaned against a pole and began to remove his shoes.

Solea glanced over and then ran to him. "What are you doing?"

"I'm the only one with the knowledge to save him. Unless I get him out, he'll die. I've been a fighter all my life. I'm not going to give up now."

"No. You'll die, too. I must be the one to save him. Tell me what to do."

"You'd never be able to. To save him requires agility and stamina. I've kept in shape all my life. I've always done the impossible. I'll bring him back to you."

Solea opened her mouth to argue, then stopped. She knew he was right, but did he still have the ability to do it?

Weiss rolled up his shirtsleeve and took a pocketknife out of his pants. He glanced nervously at the water and then sliced through his arm, dug into his skin with his fingers, and pulled out a small key. Blood dripped from the cut and onto the pavement. His legs wobbled and his vision blurred.

People around him screamed and moved away, pointing to the man who'd ripped open his arm.

Weiss looked frantically around the pier, then quickly picked up a large rock lying to the side and gripped it in his hand.

Solea grabbed his shoulder, her eyes wide with horror. "This is crazy. You're committing suicide."

Weiss stared at her for a long moment, shook her off, and then jumped from the pier and into the water.

Solea cringed as Weiss disappeared under the surface. "May God be with you both."

JACKIE GLEASON THEATER – MIAMI

The seats around Kirk filled and his exhilaration rose. He knew his father was watching over him and nothing could go wrong. He pictured tomorrow's newspaper headlines telling of the death of Houdini. Forty years ago they'd said the same, but this time the story would be true.

Once again the awesome power of the past astonished him. He felt alive and in control. Vengeance made one simple demand, and that was to succeed at all cost. He'd planned for every contingency. There would be no failure, no matter what he had to do.

A well-dressed woman with a jowly face sitting next to him leaned over. "What do you think Gleason has planned?"

Her enthusiasm annoyed him and Kirk shrugged, afraid if he spoke the woman or someone around him might recognize his voice.

"Surely you have some thoughts," she said, her smile turning to a look of confusion.

Kirk shook his head, trying to suppress his anger at this irritating woman. She looked at him strangely, then turned away. Maybe after he killed Houdini he'd shoot this woman as well.

He glanced at his watch. It was two minutes until the show started. One thing about live television was they had to be punctual.

A man in a dark suit walked on stage, stood in front of a red velvet curtain, and raised his hands to quiet the audience. "Okay folks. Mr. Gleason will be out in a couple of minutes. I know I don't have to tell you to applaud loudly when he comes out. Remember this is live television, so please don't yell things out to him. Now sit back and enjoy the show."

A moment later, the house lights dimmed and the orchestra began to play Gleason's theme song. It seemed like the entire audience leaned forward in anticipation of the comedian's appearance. Kirk tapped his knee to the beat of the music. Shortly Houdini would be dead and he'd be back in his beach house listening to Chopin or Mozart. He was about to take one step closer to his destiny.

The music stopped, the curtains parted, and the announcer said, "From the Fun and Sun Capital of the World, it's the Jackie Gleason Show." Gleason walked onto the stage. He was dressed in a black and white, plaid sport jacket and baggy gray slacks. In person he appeared even larger than he did on television, Kirk thought.

Gleason smiled and bowed as the spectators cheered loudly. When they stopped he said, "I've never been as excited about a show as I am about the one tonight. The people milling around backstage are all legends. Albert Einstein said, 'The fairest thing we can ever experience is the mysterious.' The performances you are about to witness will be miraculous. Some of what you see you won't believe. And later in the show you'll have an experience you will remember for the rest of your life."

Kirk sat back. He knew Houdini would be on last. He'd waited this long to kill him. He could wait a while longer.

17

BLOOD MIXED WITH WATER FLOATED AROUND HIS ARMS

HALLOVER PIER – MIAMI BEACH

Stanford tried not to panic. Keeping his eyes scrunched closed, he tugged on the handcuffs again. He'd practiced with them all afternoon and they'd opened easily. Could someone have tampered with them? He remembered asking for a volunteer to examine the cuffs, and the dark haired Cuban guy who'd picked them up and looked at them closely. At the time, he had a feeling the man seemed familiar, but quickly dismissed the thought. Now, submerged in water, it rushed back to him and he knew where he'd seen him before. He'd approached Solea at the Fontainebleau.

Stay calm, he thought to himself. *If you don't, you'll drown.* An eerie silence surrounded him. The wetness of his clothes and the density of the water made it difficult to move. There were a few inches at the top of the cell not filled with water, but the box was too narrow for him to maneuver in. He'd practiced holding his breath and knew he only had a few minutes before he'd be too weak to move. He had to focus on how to escape. He couldn't let this glass enclosed container become his tomb.

He flailed his arms in another vain attempt to break loose from the cuffs. His thoughts switched to Solea. She'd warned him. She had a vision he'd drown. If he got out of this, he'd always listen to her fears.

Flickering stars entered his vision and he felt like his mind was closing up. He let a little more air seep from his lungs. For the first time in his life, he felt fear. He'd been vain and egotistical, never caring if he hurt other people in his struggle to achieve his dreams. *Please, God,* he thought. *Get me out of this and I'll change. I want to do something with my life besides become famous.*

Then the cell shook and Stanford opened his eyes. The salt water stung and he blinked several times to clear his vision. For a moment, he thought he had passed out and was hallucinating. Then he realized it wasn't a mirage. A man pounded on the glass with a large rock. Blood mixed with water floated around his arms. The man's eyes narrowed, his face reddened, and a look of determination crossed his face. A few bubbles of air surrounded his head. In that instant, Stanford recognized the clean-shaven man and felt a moment of hope. If anyone could save him, it was Houdini.

Everything seemed to happen in slow motion. Houdini's hand rose in the air and descended, smashing the rock into the cell. Once, twice, a third time. Stanford shook his head slightly. It wasn't going to work. Then the glass shattered into pinpoint shards and Houdini reached in, tugging the glass away. The jagged pieces cut his fingers, but Houdini appeared unaware and worked feverishly.

He groggily sensed hands tugging his arms as black circles closed in on Stanford's vision. He felt weak and nauseous. Then a long, dark tunnel smothered his consciousness.

The water stung Houdini's eyes and a pain throbbed in his abdomen. He pulled another razor-sharp fragment of glass out and stuck his arm through the opening. He fumbled with the key, his strength ebbing with each passing second. Through the murky water he saw Stanford's head lolled to one side, his eyes closed. Houdini took the magician's limp arms, inserted the key into the handcuff lock, and twisted. Nothing happened. He tried again and it still wouldn't budge. It was then he noted that someone had jammed the lock. This had happened to him a couple of times in his career, and he knew it would take brute strength to open the cuffs.

His stomach cramped and Houdini stifled a scream of agony. Blood continued to pour from his arm and fingers, streaking skyward. At one time, he could hold his breath for a few minutes, but that was when he was younger. He needed to act quickly.

He twisted the key again, hoping it wouldn't break off in the lock. If that happened, all was lost. A searing jolt of adrenaline pushed him on. With one firm twist, the cuffs snapped loose.

Stanford's eyes opened for a moment, then flickered and closed. Houdini reached in, grabbed the magician's body under the shoulders, and tugged it. He seemed lighter than Houdini had thought. Sharp pinpricks pierced Stanford's clothes and Houdini grunted as he wrenched him through the broken glass and into the open water. He frantically pumped his arm as he tried to move upward while supporting Stanford's body. His strength lessened with each thrust.

For the first time in his life, he had a vision of his death. He pictured his mother's face, and then Bess. He shoved Stanford away from him. Maybe the magician could save himself.

Stanford's gaze darted back and forth. Houdini pointed toward the surface. Stanford shook his head, reached out, and moved toward Houdini as if trying to help him. Houdini waved him off and backed away. Stanford stared at him for a few seconds, then his body twisted and started to head up. The magician flailed his arms, righted himself, and floated toward the surface.

Houdini saw a shimmer of light as he looked skyward. He had saved Stanford and now he must fight to survive. This was truly the greatest moment of his life. No feeling was greater than saving the life of another.

He'd always been a good swimmer. He'd get out of this. Then his stomach cramped again. He tried to push off the ocean bottom, but his legs didn't have enough strength. In the distance he saw a long, dark tunnel. On both sides of it were cheering crowds and at the end stood Bess, looking more beautiful than ever. She held her arms out to him. His thoughts drifted, and he pictured himself as he had been many years ago—young, strong, and performing illusions in front of thousands of adoring fans. Then he saw his mother, standing next to Bess with her arms outstretched. As the darkness surrounded him, he took a step toward them. He could feel himself smiling.

Kirk watched Jackie Gleason's tuxedo jacket pull tight around his waist as he bent to do a fancy dance step. The comedian tossed his cane into the air and caught it flawlessly. Scantily clad women glided around him moving gracefully, in sharp contrast to Gleason's fumbling moves. Gleason knocked the top hat from his head and caught it in his hand. The audience cheered as the routine ended.

Kirk fidgeted in his seat surprised by the nervousness he felt. What was Gleason waiting for? He thought. Why the delay? He'd sat restlessly through a few old magicians' routines in stoic silence, his mind focused on his mission.

Gleason wiped sweat from his brow and then swept his arm toward the women as they left the stage. "Have you enjoyed the show so far?" He hesitated as the audience applauded. "Well, I've got one more special guest for you, and I do mean special. I'm sure you've heard rumors about something spectacular happening tonight. Get ready. You are not going to believe what you see."

Kirk sat forward and loosened his sport jacket so he could reach his gun easily.

Gleason looked toward the wings as if in anticipation. An irritated expression crossed his face for an instant. Then he turned to the audience. "I'm glad so many of my friends are here tonight for this amazing event." A few people waved from the audience, but Kirk sat still. "I've got a few more backstage, and they'll be out after the grand finale." Gleason shifted his weight. "In just a few moments what you'll witness is going to knock you, bang zoom, right to the moon, as I always tell Alice."

A stagehand walked onto the stage and whispered in Gleason's ear.

The comedian's face whitened for an instant and then he smiled. "For the people at home, we're going to cut to a commercial, but don't you dare go away. They'll be worth sitting through for the extraordinary event you are about to see."

Something was wrong. Kirk could sense it. His gaze darted left and right checking the exits to make sure nothing would block his escape.

Two men came onto the stage and huddled with Gleason. Finger jabs and animated talking punctuated the conversation. Gleason appeared upset as he walked off.

Kirk focused on the slow rhythm of his breathing, trying to remain calm. His moment of justice was about to take place. He was sure he'd get away, but if getting caught was the price to pay, so be it.

Loud talking came from behind the closed curtain and the audience quieted to hear the words. Kirk leaned forward, but the words were muffled. Maybe Houdini had backed out and Gleason was arguing with him now. Kirk's instincts told him everything would go smoothly. His father's words drifted into his consciousness. Houdini will die tonight.

Out of the corner of his eye, he noticed a policeman coming through the exit on his right. Another followed him out. They seemed to be staring directly at Kirk. Two other officers entered from the opposite side.

They approached him, the overhead lights shining on the brim of their caps. "Would you come with us, sir," one said quietly.

Kirk's heart hammered. People around him quieted and turned to stare. The jowly woman's expression said, I knew there was something strange about him.

Kirk smiled. There was no way for them to know what he had planned. "For what reason, officer?"

"We need to talk to you about a serious matter."

Kirk noted the television camera swivel and point toward him. He knew, at that moment, his image was being broadcast nationwide. "Can't we do it right here? I don't want to miss the rest of the show."

"It'll be easier if you come with us."

Kirk got up, his anger rising. "Do you know who I am?" The second the words left his mouth, he realized he was in disguise. How could he explain the way he was dressed?

"Yes, sir," the officer said. "You're Anthony Kirk."

Kirk's mind tumbled. How could they possibly know? He had to remain calm or all was lost.

"Would you open your jacket, please?"

"Certainly not. This is outrageous. If you know who I am then you know I can have your badge taken away. This is harassment. What is it I'm supposed to have done?"

The officer ignored the question. "From the bulge in your coat it looks to me as if you're carrying a weapon."

The television camera moved closer. "I've committed no crime."

The two cops exchanged a look that Kirk couldn't read. "We sent men to your home. They told us about the threats to

133

Houdini in blood written on your wall. Mr. Gleason just confirmed that the magician is scheduled to be on his show tonight."

"Searched my house? On what grounds? You had no right."

"Your niece called us. She told us some very interesting things. She lived with you at one time, didn't she?"

Kirk didn't respond.

"You admitted to her you were behind the attempt on Rabbi Weiss's life and that you intended to kill Houdini tonight in front of a live television audience."

"I did nothing of the kind. My niece is crazy. Always having these visions. She's the one you should be questioning."

"Funny thing is, when we talked to her on the phone she told us exactly what seat you'd be sitting in and that you'd be in a disguise. How do you think she knew that? Did you leave the ticket and make up kit out for her to find? Not too bright for a smart man like you."

There was a sudden movement off to his right. A cop pushed closer and the two in front of him seemed confused. Then gunshots exploded. One, two, and a third, so close it felt like the floor shook. The two policemen's eyes widened and a look of panic crossed their faces. Kirk felt a sharp pain in his chest. He looked down and saw blood spurting from a wound near his heart. The last two things Kirk saw as black consciousness enveloped him were the television camera swooping closer and Jose Ramirez, disguised as a Miami cop, being grabbed and the gun torn from his fingers.

18
STANFORD'S TALL TALE

Larry King studied the two people seated beside him. It was a coup to get them on his show. The publicity that had surrounded the pair during the past several months was immense and that they'd decided to break their silence on his program was a tribute not so much to him but to their love for the city of Miami.

The mystery surrounding the death of Rabbi Weiss, as well as the specifics of the show Gleason had planned on magicians, had intensified since the events occurred and the key principals had remained mute. King hoped to be able to find out some new information from Stanford.

"Our special guests tonight are The Great Stanford and his new bride, Solea. Welcome to the show, and congratulations on your marriage."

"Thanks, Larry. Having our wedding at the Fontainebleau where I proposed was special enough, but when Sinatra showed up and sang a few songs it was beyond belief."

Solea leaned toward the microphone. "He asked me to sing a song with him, but I declined."

King grinned. "Sinatra's not used to people saying no, so you better watch out." He cleared his throat. "You've had some strange things happen to you during the last several months. Let's get right to them."

Stanford squeezed Solea's hand. "Yes, we did, and we want

135

all our fans to know we're both fine and will be back to performing shortly. The cards and letters we've received have been amazing. By the way, from now on I'll be performing simply under the name Stanford."

King glanced at Solea's swollen belly. "And I can see you are about to become proud parents. It looks like you're going to be looking for a new assistant, Stanford. When is the baby due?"

Solea patted her stomach. "We hope the baby will arrive on Halloween. If it's a boy we'll name it Harry and, if a girl, Bess."

"It would be fitting if the child arrived on Halloween. As everyone knows, Stanford is a great admirer of Harry Houdini and has promised to tell us about the rumors that have been swirling since last Halloween. Not even Gleason, who you usually can't shut up, will talk about it. Could you shed any light on what occurred that night?"

"I can, and I feel it's time to set things straight. I made this promise to Houdini himself."

King frowned. "Houdini? You're far too young to have personally talked to Houdini."

"But I have." He glanced at Solea. "We both have."

"You mean you've spoken to him through a psychic? Why hasn't anyone heard about this?"

"No, Larry. I talked to the man himself."

King sat back and for the first time in many years was at a loss for words. He didn't like to confront his guests, but what Stanford was saying was ridiculous.

"Are you saying Houdini isn't dead? Because if you are I refuse to believe you. Sure, there were rumors floating around that he had faked his death, but that would be impossible. Most people felt it was just a publicity stunt done by friends who didn't want Houdini to be forgotten. You may be a great magician, but I don't think you could bring Houdini back from the grave."

"Unfortunately Houdini is dead now, but he didn't die forty years ago as most people thought. For all that time he hid out in Miami. Here he was known as Rabbi Weiss and only a few knew his real identity. He died nine months ago while trying to save my life."

A bead of sweat creased King's forehead. Why hadn't his producer told him Stanford was going to tell this unbelievable story? Tomorrow he'd be ridiculed across the country for allowing this to happen. He had to pull the plug on this interview.

He pointed to his producer. "We're going to cut to a commercial break."

King got up and huddled with his producer in a corner. "Get a recording of one of our old shows to fill up the rest of the hour. I'm going to tape what Stanford has to say. I don't believe a word of it, but if it's any good we can broadcast it tomorrow night."

"Are you sure about this, Larry?" the producer asked.

"My reputation's on the line here. I'm not about to have some crackpot make a fool out of me on live radio. As far as Stanford's concerned, he's still on the air. Let's hear what he has to say."

When King returned to the table, he placed a Wollensak recorder in the middle. "You don't mind if we make a back up tape, do you? We just want to make sure we get everything you say."

"Not at all," Stanford said.

"Thirty seconds," the producer said.

King jabbed a finger at Stanford. "Look, you can't come on this show and make ludicrous statements like this."

"They're not ludicrous. If you allow the show to continue I'll prove what I'm saying is true. Rabbi Weiss was a great man who did many wonderful things for those less fortunate. Few knew his real identity. Now, his friends want the truth told." Stanford pointed toward a booth on the other side of the room.

King's jaw dropped when he saw Jackie Gleason seated next to Karen Bonanno, Weiss's housekeeper. He recognized her from the pictures that had appeared in the paper after the Rabbi's death.

"When I've finished telling my story they've agreed to come on the show and verify everything I've said."

"You're on," the producer said.

King pressed the play button on the recorder. "Welcome back to the Larry King Show. This may turn out to be one of our strangest shows. Our guest is Stanford, the magician who claims to be Houdini's protégée. He just made a startling revelation about Houdini not dying in 1926. Stanford, can you back up your claim?"

"First, I'd like to say what a great man Harry Houdini was. In the past few months I've reevaluated what I want to do with my life." He squeezed Solea's hand. "Yeah, I'll continue to do magic, but I want more than fame. I need to help people the way Houdini did during the last forty years of his life. I also want to honor his memory. Karen Bonanno, his housekeeper for the last forty years, was left all of Houdini's props in his will. She in turn has given them to me. I'm going to open a museum to honor the world's greatest magician. Karen has agreed to run the museum and will talk about her plans for it later in this show. In a few minutes, Jackie Gleason will tell you that Houdini was scheduled to appear live on his program and about his friendship with the man. Houdini never made it to the theater because he lost his life trying to save me from drowning."

"You'll have to excuse me if I'm in shock, and I'm sure my listeners are having trouble believing what you're saying, too."

"Well, then, sit back, Mr. King. I have an amazing tale to tell, and it's about time everyone knew it. I'm going to honor Houdini's last request to me, by telling why he faked his death forty years ago and why he decided to reveal his identity after all that time. It's a sad story. One based on greed and deception. It all started forty years ago when people assumed it was Houdini who died trying to perform the Water Cell Torture Escape."

Stanford noticed a wisp of fog seeping in through an open window of the restaurant. It moved closer and hovered over Larry King's shoulder. Stanford smiled, and then started to tell his story.

WOLFIE'S DELI – LATER THAT NIGHT

The darkened restaurant was closed and locked up tight. On the table, next to a microphone, sat Larry King's Wollensak tape recorder. A translucent strip of fog seeped under the door, floated across the room, and hovered over the machine. The photos on the wall shook slightly.

The fog blanketed the reel to reel. It suddenly snapped on and garbled voices at super fast speed filled the air. Then the tape broke and caught fire as the reel flipped out of the machine onto the floor. The flickering flames consumed the tape and then quickly the blaze went out, leaving the restaurant in total darkness and the reel destroyed.

THE END